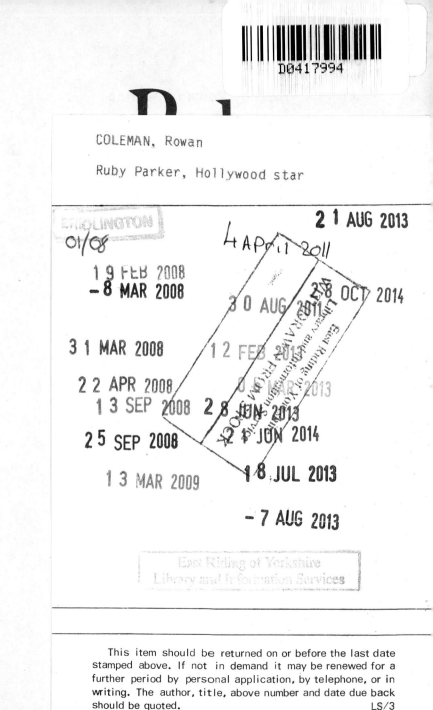

This item should be returned on or before the last date stamped above. If not in demand it may be renewed for a further period by personal application, by telephone, or in writing. The author, title, above number and date due back should be quoted.   LS/3

Also by Rowan Coleman

Ruby Parker: Soap Star
Ruby Parker: Film Star

Ruby Parker

Hollywood Star

ROWAN COLEMAN

HarperCollins *Children's Books*

First published in Great Britain by HarperCollins *Children's Books* 2007
HarperCollins *Children's Books* is a division of HarperCollins*Publishers* Ltd
77-85 Fulham Palace Road, Hammersmith, London W6 8JB

www.harpercollinschildrensbooks.co.uk

I

Text copyright © Rowan Coleman 2007.

The author asserts the moral right to be
identified as the author of this work.

ISBN-13 978-0-00-724433-1
ISBN-10 0-00-724433-9

Printed and bound in England by
Clays Ltd, St Ives plc

From: Ruby (rparker@beverlyhills.com)

To: Nydia (nassimin@breakaleg.co.uk);
Danny (dharvey@breakaleg.co.uk);
Annie (amchance@breakaleg.co.uk);
Sean: (srivers@breakaleg.co.uk)

Subject: Hello! From Hollywood!

Hi guys!

Well, I'm here in Beverly Hills! We got here yesterday night and I still haven't properly got over the long flight, the first time I've ever flown this far. It makes me feel all fuzzy and backwards. I couldn't sleep on the plane even though we flew first class and there were beds and everything, I was so excited! You wouldn't believe Jeremy's house (well, Anne-Marie and Sean might)! It's gigantic! I don't even know how big because all I've done since I got here is sleep and have breakfast and e-mail you lot. But I can tell you that I have my own bathroom, sitting room, complete with TV and laptop in my bedroom. Which in my opinion makes it more like a house than just a room, but anyway the house is in the hills above L.A. and I can even see the Hollywood sign from the window.

It seems like a lot of house to have when Jeremy isn't even here half the time, but I suppose that's what you do when you've made it big in Hollywood. Spend all your money on stuff. It still feels weird to see Mum and Jeremy "together", holding hands and being all soppy. It was even weirder to leave Dad and Everest at Christmas, especially as me and Dad sort of fell out before I left. I think he is less OK about Mum and Jeremy than he makes out, especially since his so-called girlfriend chucked him.

Anyway this is my first proper morning in America and I am very excited. It is warm out (weird for December) and the sky is blue.

Miss you all

Rubesx ☺

Chapter One

When I opened my eyes this
morning I had that holiday feeling,
times about one million.

RUBY PARKER

I always get it when I sleep in a new place. I was so
used to looking at the same ceiling, and the same books
on the shelves and posters on the walls, that when I
opened my eyes I felt a little rush of excitement when I
remembered exactly where I was. Sometimes when I was
little, after Mum and Dad had kissed me goodnight, I
used to put my pillow at the wrong end of the bed and
sleep upside down so that when I woke up everything
would be topsy-turvy and for a minute I'd have that
holiday feeling.

But on my first morning in Jeremy's Fort's Hollywood
home it wasn't only that supercharged holiday feeling I
had: it felt like I was stepping out of my life and into a
movie.

I have made a film now and it's nothing like you think
it's going to be. Every day is long and most of the time
you spend waiting around to do your scene, which you

usually have to do several times with lots more waiting around in between, and sometimes you can't even remember where you are in the plot. Sometimes, in fact a lot of the time, making a film is quite boring. So when I say waking up in a movie, I don't mean waking up on a film set. I mean that on my first morning at Jeremy's house I felt like I had been zapped right through a cinema screen and straight into a living, breathing fantasy land. Although I knew it was real and that I really was in Hollywood, everything I looked at in my room that morning seemed a little bit shinier, a little more special than it did back at home. It was like the old musicals that Mum loves watching; the colours were deeper and brighter, and at any minute I got the feeling that everyone would stop what they were doing and burst into song.

I wasn't surprised because this is Hollywood, and if this is the town where dreams comes true, then it made sense to me that being here would be like living in a Technicolor dream.

It was certainly a change after the year I've had, which has been amazing but exhausting and quite confusing; the year when I stopped being properly a kid any more and really started to grow up. The biggest thing that happened was that Dad stopped living at home and now my parents are divorcing. That was and *is* the hardest thing for me to get used to, but Mum and Dad seem to have moved on so fast that I almost feel I have to run to catch up with them. Sometimes I wonder if they are actually running away from the past instead of running *towards* the future. But I haven't said anything to either of them because they both seem quite happy now, especially Mum.

In the middle of Dad leaving home I had my first proper storyline in top telly soap opera *Kensington Heights*, my first fake kiss from co-star Justin de Souza and my first real kiss from Danny Harvey, who is now my boyfriend. And then I left *Kensington Heights* to "find myself", and found myself with a part in the Hollywood movie *The Lost Treasure of King Arthur*, directed by Art Dubrovnik and starring double Oscar winner Imogene Grant and leading British actor Jeremy Fort. I made friends with teen heart-throb and movie mega star Sean Rivers, rescued him from his evil father and helped reunite him with his long lost mum. Now he lives with her in London and goes to my school, Sylvia Lighthouse's Academy for the Performing Arts. And on top of *that*, my best friend Nydia collapsed and hit her head very hard because she'd decided to stop eating to try and lose weight quickly.

But the weirdest thing of all was that my mum and Jeremy Fort started going out together! And that is properly weird because my mum is my *mum*. She's pretty but she's not glamorous or amazingly beautiful, or a Russian supermodel like Jeremy's last girlfriend Carenza Slavchenkov, but it seems as if they are getting quite serious, because here we all are at his Hollywood home for the Christmas holidays.

Like I said, *weird*.

When I finally got up I had a shower, got dressed, then ventured outside of my bedroom to find Mum and Jeremy. I felt nervous about leaving my room, all fizzy and fluttery inside. I wasn't sure what was going to happen during my two week holiday from my normal life, but I felt sure that they would be the most special, most exciting, most fun two weeks ever!

The house was covered from head to foot in the kinds of Christmas decorations that you usually only ever see in shops like Harrods. The banister was entwined with thick fake pine bunting, encrusted with glittering baubles that reflected the morning sunlight so brightly they almost dazzled me as I came down the grand staircase. In the hallway stood a Christmas tree that had to be nearly as big as the one the Norwegians give us Brits every year to put up in Trafalgar Square. It had an interestingly large amount of presents stacked underneath. I wondered if they were real gifts or fake ones like you get in department stores. As I studied them I noticed a furry little face with beady eyes peeping out from behind one especially big present. I hoped that it wasn't a present for me because as a girl of nearly fourteen I was pretty much over cuddly toys, a fact that even basic research of my interests would have alerted him to. I was just rehearsing the appropriate polite and pleased response when suddenly the creature leapt straight at me.

I screamed my head off.

"It's a rat! A rat, a rat is biting me!" I shrieked as it grabbed my trouser leg and began to shake and tug at it vigorously, almost pulling me off balance. Mum, Jeremy, Jeremy's chef Augusto and Marie the housekeeper all came racing into the hall. But instead of saving me from the mutant rodent, they all stopped in their tracks, smiling, and Mum even *laughed*.

"*David!*" Jeremy said sharply. "Come, boy."

I stood in awe as the rat with a name stopped yanking at my trouser leg. Giving me a haughty look, it trotted over to Jeremy and leapt up into his arms. It was then that I noticed it had a collar. I knew Hollywood was a place where weird fads ruled, that some film stars had pigs for pets and others kept snakes, but I honestly thought that Jeremy was far too sensible to put a collar on a rat and call it David.

"Silly girl," Mum said, reaching out and ruffling David's head. "Since when do rats bark? This is Jeremy's Chihuahua. He's a dog, silly."

I stared at the creature who was watching me intently from Jeremy's arms. Of course he was a dog. I'd seen dogs like him before when we watched Crufts and also quite often peeping out from the specially made handbags of hotel heiresses, wearing diamond-encrusted ribbons. It was just that everything had happened so quickly I'd put two and two together and made eight. Besides, it was the last kind of pet that I expected Jeremy to have.

"Sorry," I said, feeling the heat in my cheeks. "I didn't mean to call your dog a rat."

Jeremy laughed. "Don't worry, Ruby. When I first set eyes on him that's exactly what I thought too. He used to belong to the young woman who lives a few houses down. But when it became more fashionable to have a lamb on a lead she kicked poor old David out into the street without a second thought. He found his way here so Marie and I decided to give him a home. When you get to know him he's really quite a character. I'm sure you'll be great friends."

Gingerly, I reached out a hand and tried to pat David on the head. He bared his needly little teeth at me and snarled. I wasn't sure I agreed with Jeremy.

"David's a funny name for a dog," I said, withdrawing fingers quickly.

"I call him David because despite his tiny size he's prepared to take on any Goliath in a fight. He's got a lion's heart." Jeremy grinned and nodded towards the kitchen. "So, let's have breakfast and plan our first day together in Hollywood."

David looked at me from over Jeremy's shoulder and for a second I wondered if the film of my life had turned into a Disney cartoon. Because I could have sworn that the evil little dog was laughing at me.

As I entered the kitchen I had to stop myself for a second by a fridge the size of a car and take a breath at what I saw. There was my mum, with quite a lot of grey roots showing in her hair and wearing some jogging bottoms from Primark, sitting holding Jeremy Fort's hand with one hand and eating a grapefruit with the other.

That was when it hit me.

This is my life now. My mum is going out with someone properly famous and rich, and I have just made a film with him due to be released really soon, which means that before long I might be properly famous too, not just in Britain – but all over the world. I felt my knees buckle and it seemed as if I had forgotten how to breathe out.

School, Dad and Everest, and even Danny and Nydia seemed very far away from me, and I felt homesick and scared, excited and thrilled all at once. This holiday was going to be just a taste of what my life might turn into. This lifestyle, this kind of house, even this stupid dog with a stupid name could be the sort of thing that I take for granted in a few short weeks when my film comes out. If the last year had been a rollercoaster, I couldn't imagine what heights the next year might hold for me.

"Well," Jeremy said as he finished eating breakfast, "I have to confess that I've been so busy with this new shoot that I haven't bought any gifts yet, so as today is Christmas Eve and time is running out I've decided I'm taking you two ladies shopping. You can choose whatever you want – so start thinking!"

"Oh Jeremy, you don't have to do that," my mum said happily. "We don't expect you to buy us expensive presents."

"Don't we?" I said, a bit disappointed that all the presents under the tree must be fake after all. Mum raised a warning brow at me and Jeremy laughed.

"It feels funny enough as it is," Mum went on. "Having someone else doing all the cleaning and the cooking and even the Christmas dinner! I hope you don't think that the reason I... we... Ruby and I... are friends with you is because of all this. I mean, I knew you'd done well, but I honestly had no idea that you were quite so... well... rich."

"My dear Janice," Jeremy said, and he actually picked my mum's hand up and *kissed* it, "I think you and I both know why we have become 'friends' and it had nothing to do with the mere trappings of wealth. Besides, if you don't want expensive presents, then don't choose expensive presents."

"But the option is there to go expensive, right?" I said just to make my mum's eyes flash.

Jeremy smiled at me. "I can't remember the last time I had a proper Christmas like this one, with people that I care for. I never married, never had children. What family I have is far away and distant. So you and your mum's gift to me this year is your company, and giving me the pleasure of making your stay a happy one."

"So *we* don't actually have to buy *you* anything?" I asked mischievously.

"Ruby!" my mum exclaimed. "Remember you manners."

"It's fine, Janice," Jeremy said. "I think my old friend Ruby here is teasing. Besides, it would be difficult to find inexpensive gifts where we are going."

"Where *are* we going?" I asked.

"Rodeo Drive. The most glamorous shopping street in the world. What do say, Ruby?"

I grinned at my mum. "I say, let's go shopping!"

Somewhere between leaving in Jeremy's silver Rolls Royce and returning five hours later, my mum had forgotten entirely that she didn't want anything from him at all except his "friendship".

I've never really done designer labels, not because I didn't want to but because I wasn't allowed to in case I got spoiled. (I should be so lucky.) It seemed, however, that the same rules did not apply to mums who date film stars and even I recognised the labels on the bags that she came back with: Armani, Gucci, Donna Karan, to name just a few. All names of people who make a lot of money selling posh stuff that from a not very great distance looks exactly the same as stuff from Marks and Spencer or Asda. But anyway, it made Mum really happy. In fact, more than happy – she was sparkly and excited, like *she* was the teenager let loose with a credit card and not me.

Surprisingly, I found it much harder to spend Jeremy's money. I kept thinking about my dad and the last time I had seen him, the night before we flew out. I had gone round to his flat to give him instructions for looking after my cat Everest. I also took the present I'd bought for him, which was a DIY manual because he still hasn't done up his flat, and it's all miserable and grey and old ladyish.

He looked miserable too when I went in – like he had started to blend in with his surroundings. He made me a hot chocolate and we sat on the lumpy old sofa.

"Are you still OK about me going?" I asked, because he wasn't talking.

He gave me a sort of unhappy smile and said, "Of course I am."

"You'll be all right," I said, leaning my head on his shoulder. "You'll have a nice lunch at Granny's with

Uncle Pete and all that lot, won't you? You love Granny's roasties."

"It's not the same though, Rube," Dad said heavily.

At first I felt guilty, but then I realised that if it was up to me, this Christmas would have been exactly like the last. Me, Mum and Dad sitting round the kitchen table in paper hats, and Everest trying to get a great big turkey leg through the cat flap without anyone noticing. Christmas was always good in our house even when Mum and Dad weren't getting on so well. It was like in the First World War when all the soldiers stopped fighting on Christmas Day and played football instead. Mum and Dad stopped arguing and pulled crackers, and we laughed at the terrible jokes because we wanted to laugh and we didn't care if they weren't funny.

And I suppose I knew last year, and even the year before that, that they were only trying for my sake, but I was glad they did it, because it meant that they were putting me first. I've been doing OK about Mum and Dad splitting up, but thinking about the kind of Christmas I would never have again made me feel cross and sad all at once.

"But, Dad," I'd said, "it wouldn't have been the same. Christmas wouldn't have been us all together anyway, would it?"

Dad shrugged so that my head bumped on his shoulder. I sat up. "I know that," he said shortly. "But I didn't imagine that I wouldn't be able to see you at all because you'd be in America with your mum's new boyfriend."

I looked at him. "So that's what you really mind," I said, my voice quite sharp. "You mind Mum having a boyfriend."

"It does feel a bit strange, Ruby," he said. "That's all."

"Well," I said, and maybe I did sound a little bit more "I told you so" than I meant to. "You're the one who wanted to break up, Dad. Me and Mum didn't. And it's not our fault if your so-called girlfriend chucked you and Mum's going out with a movie star."

"So *that's* how it is, is it?"

Dad's shout was unexpected and I jumped as he stood up so that a little bit of hot chocolate slopped out of my mug and on to my trousers. I hadn't realised he was so upset.

"That's how what is, Dad?" I said, standing too.

"You and your mum against me." Dad sounded bitter.

"No!" I started to feel cross. "No, Dad, that's *not* how it is. It's *you* that wanted to go. It's *you* that wanted to be on your own and have a so-called girlfriend. It's you, Dad, who didn't even *think* about how Christmas would be for me and Mum when you left us. I suppose you'd be happy if all we were doing was sitting around an empty table, just the two of us, feeling miserable and missing you! Would that cheer you up?"

"You used to be such a sweet little thing," Dad said and he looked at me as if he didn't know me. "But you've changed."

"It wasn't me that changed, Dad!" I shouted. "It was my life and you changed it. All I'm doing is my best to live with those changes, and if you don't like me, then, well then... I'll be gone tomorrow!"

And I ran out of his flat and slammed the door and ran back home. And I sat outside for quite a long time, cried for a bit and wondered how it was that my dad, with his terrible jokes and silly hair, had got so angry with me for something that he had done. It wasn't fair. And then I wiped my tears, put on a smile and went indoors. I didn't want Mum to know we had argued. She was feeling bad enough about taking me away for Christmas as it was.

"Your dad phoned," Mum said as I went upstairs to double-check my packing. "He says he forgot to say something to you."

"I'll ring him later," I said. But I didn't.

And for all of the eleven-hour flight, and most of

yesterday and last night and this morning, I didn't feel bad about it at all. It was only when Jeremy started buying us presents that I felt awkward, as if accepting gifts that Dad could never have afforded to give me or Mum in a million years was taking me another step further away from him.

So all I got was an iPod, three dresses, two pairs of jeans, some trainers and a great big pair of sunglasses with little diamantes sparkling round the rims, just like you see real film stars wearing on TV. Well. I thought it would be rude not to get anything, even though my heart wasn't really in it.

As we got back in Jeremy's car I put the sunglasses on with the tag still attached and flapping in my face. Then I rolled down the window and shouted, "Watch out, Hollywood, here comes Ruby Parker!"

I expected Mum to tell me off, but she didn't. She was too busy looking in her shopping bags and gazing adoringly at Jeremy. I pushed the button to close the window and put her unusual lapse in making sure I kept my feet firmly on the ground down to jet lag and excitement. After all, it had been a mad day. People stopped Jeremy every few minutes, some to get his autograph but more because they knew him, worked with him or were extremely famous themselves. We even got followed by the paparazzi for a bit and they took Jeremy's photo, and even mine and Mum's, when we went for lunch.

Mum and I thought it was rather funny to be followed around by press photographers when they couldn't have known who we were. We made a game of changing hats, sunglasses and tops as we went from shop to shop, getting snapped in a new outfit each time we came out.

"Just ignore them," Jeremy told us. "They take photos of me but they never get printed. I'm far too boring to make a tabloid story."

And after a while the photographers disappeared in search of the snap that would earn them their fortune. I didn't think I'd ever see one of the photos they took of us in print.

But I was wrong.

People's Choice Magazine

We love the English, and especially those Hollywood Brits. For years now *IN THE KNOW* has admired one Brit in particular, legendary actor Jeremy Fort. But is it possible that Mr Fort has recently lost the plot (just like his latest action movie)?

Yes, it's incredible but true – *IN THE KNOW* can exclusively reveal that Jeremy Fort has ditched stunning supermodel Carenza Slavchenkov for a British mom and we're not talking Madonna! (*photo top left*).

Our sources tell us that Janice Parker is the mother of English child actress wannabe Ruby Parker who features alongside Fort in the soon to be released *The Lost Treasure of King Arthur.* (And the studio's hoping it *does* get lost!) Apparently, an on-set friendship soon turned to romance over tea and English muffins, and good old Jerry has brought his ready-made family to La-La Land for the holidays. *IN*

THE KNOW can confirm he was really splashing the cash on Ruby and her mom on Christmas Eve to the tune of $10,000.

It just goes to show that the British are the most eccentric race in the world. Only an Englishman would swap leggy lovely Carenza for a middle-aged fashion-disaster nobody. Perhaps next time you get out your credit card, Jeremy, you should treat Mrs Parker to a little nip and tuck for New Year?

Then again, perhaps other old Brit, William Shakespeare, summed it up best when he said, "Love is blind!"

Chapter Two

The first week in Hollywood passed in a flash. Before I knew it, it was nearly New Year's Eve.

Until then Christmas had been nice. Or perhaps I should say wonderful because of all the effort that Jeremy and Augusto and Marie put in. But the best I can say is nice, because it was so different from the kind of Christmas I was used to and it would have taken a lot longer than one day to get used to it.

It wasn't at all like being at home with Mum and Dad and Everest. Mum always used to insist that we all opened only one present before breakfast and then saved the rest till after lunch. But not in Jeremy's house. We opened all the presents at once, first thing in the morning, creating a whirlwind of shiny paper and ribbon and lots of glittery sparkles that drove David mad.

The Chihuahua even had several gifts of his own, most of which were food-based. One was a sort of royal-blue satin throne bed with a little gold-painted wooden staircase leading up to the mattress. But David was more interested in ripping up the paper than lounging on the bed, which made him seem a bit more dog-like and a lot less evil nemesis.

As I opened my gifts I found the things I had picked out on Rodeo Drive and a whole lot more besides that somehow Mum and Jeremy had chosen without me knowing. Clothes, shoes – some even with a low heel and a bit of a pointy toe – and best of all a make-up set. I stared open-mouthed at my mum who never, ever let me wear make-up except for work or the occasional event.

"That's from me," she said with a smile. "I thought it was about time you had something to practise with. But not to be worn outside the house unless I say so, OK?"

"OK, Mum," I said and immediately put on some green sparkly eyeshadow. I didn't look exactly how Anne-Marie did when she wore it, but I was happy anyway.

And then Mum handed me something she had brought from home. I could tell because it was wrapped in normal penguin-in-a-bobble-hat Christmas paper, not covered in tons of ribbons and bows.

"From your dad," she said. I took a breath and opened it.

It was a blue top from Miss Selfridge that I had shown Dad the last time we went out for lunch. I looked at it and suddenly I realised how much I missed him. My dad who went into a girls' shop to buy a top he especially knew I wanted all on his own with no one to help him. The top probably cost a fraction of any of the other gifts that I had, but along with my make-up set it was the best one there.

I wanted to ring Dad and thank him. I looked at my watch and then at my mum. It was just after ten in the morning here so it would be about teatime at home.

"Go on," she said with a smile. "Call him and say Happy Christmas from me too."

But when I dialled Dad's number the phone just rang and rang, and I imagined his horrible, cold, empty grey flat all those thousands of miles away echoing with the sound. I tried his mobile next, but that went to voicemail. I supposed he couldn't hear it at Granny's. I didn't leave a message because I thought that after the last time we spoke a message wasn't right, so I padded back downstairs.

After presents came Christmas lunch. It was a bit like I imagine having Christmas at Buckingham Palace would be and was about as different from lunch at home as it could be. Jeremy's dining room, with its mile-long shiny wooden table that could seat about thirty, was a universe apart from our kitchen table with the wobbly leg and the giant cat permanently installed under it in the hopes of pinching scraps. David did race up and down underneath the table, yapping for treats and nipping toes, but it wasn't the same. I wondered what Everest would think of David and I decided that he would probably eat him.

Lunch was delicious though. Augusto and Marie, who were married but didn't have any children yet, ate with us, which was really nice. The adults drank champagne and Augusto turned out to be very funny, telling us all about the famous neighbours and what they get up to when they think no one is looking. When I asked him how he knew all of these stories he looked very solemn and told me it was Chef's Code and he could not reveal his sources.

"When chefs get together they are like a bunch of old women gossiping," Marie said, chuckling.

After lunch Jeremy took us for a walk around his gardens. I trailed a little bit behind as he and Mum walked on ahead hand in hand, while David ran in and out of his legs, threatening to trip him up. They really did look comfortable, like a couple who had been together for years. It was strange: the more time I spent with Jeremy like this, off a film set and just sort of hanging about with him, the less I saw him as that dynamic, daring actor I admired so much. I mean I still admired and looked up to him, but it was like he was splitting into two people. Famous Jeremy Fort, former dater of supermodels, and just Jeremy, my mum's middle-aged, slightly balding, easy-going boyfriend. If he had been an accountant he would have been a lot easier to get used to.

By the time I went to bed I was exhausted, but also glad that the day was over. Because as nice as it had been, I still missed that last Christmas with Mum and Dad and the stupid paper hats and Mum trying not to swear when the turkey wasn't cooked on time. I wished I'd known it was going to be the last one we'd all have as a proper family, because I would have been more careful to remember every detail.

Just before I went to sleep I thought about trying to phone Dad again, but I decided it would be too early in the morning at home, so instead I climbed into my massive bed and stared at the ceiling. Then, after a while, I took all my pillows and piled them down at the bottom of the bed. I decided to sleep upside down. Perhaps it would help me get that holiday feeling back again.

It wasn't until New Year's Eve that we saw the column about Mum and Jeremy in *People's Choice Magazine*. After a week of sightseeing and more shopping trips, we were having a quiet day before Mum and Jeremy went out to a party at a neighbour's house. (And by neighbour I mean Catherine Zeta-Jones!) I had been invited but I decided to stay at home with Marie and Augusto, because as exciting as it might have been to get dressed up and see how many famous people I could spot (a lot), when it came down to it, it would still be an adult party with no one there for me to talk to. And Augusto and Marie were a lot of fun, plus Marie promised to make me her extra-special hot chocolate drink to toast the New Year in, if I could stay up that late. I said I'd try.

In fact, Mum and I had been picking out a dress for her to wear when we found out about the article. We might not have seen it at all (and things would have been so different if we hadn't) except for Jeremy's publicist, Michael White. I'd seen him around before on the set of *The Lost Treasure of King Arthur*, but I never really paid any attention to him because Jeremy seemed to think of him as more of a necessity than a boon and much preferred to deal with Lisa Wells, who was assistant director on the shoot. We were all in the main living area, with Mum parading up and down in various frocks, Jeremy reading through scripts and giving us his opinion every now and then, and me pretending that I was Tyra Banks on *America's Next Top Old Model* when the doorbell chimed 'God Save the Queen'. David went bananas, flying at the door like a four-legged spitfire.

Jeremy sighed when he realised it was Michael and he apologised to us as he got up and went to greet him. I noticed he let David nip at Michael's ankles for quite a long time before calling the tiny dog off.

I watched them out of the corner of my eye while Mum tried to pick accessories for a bright pink silk dress that was her current favourite. Michael and Jeremy were talking as if they didn't want anybody to hear what they were saying, their heads close together. Then Michael handed Jeremy a magazine and watched as he read it, rubbing his chin with his hand. Jeremy's face grew red and he threw the magazine across the polished tiled floor so that it skidded to a stop by my mum's feet.

"Ridiculous rag!" he bellowed. "This is outrageous. Janice isn't a celebrity – she's not putting herself in the spotlight! How dare they attack her?"

"Me?" Mum said with a puzzled smile. She put down the evening bag she had been carrying and picked up the magazine. Her eyes widened as she took in what she saw there.

"What is it, Mum?" I asked, but she just stared at the magazine, her confusion turning into a look of horror.

Jeremy came and put his arm around her stiff shoulders. "Janice, I'm so sorry…"

"Perhaps," Michael said, walking a few steps nearer, "they think that by dating you, Janice is putting herself in the public eye and making herself fair game."

Frustrated, I took the magazine from Mum's frozen fingers and read the column for myself.

"Look, Jeremy," Michael went on, "as irritating and unkind as that is, what the studio and I are really worried about are those other comments. The press have already got it in for *The Lost Treasure of King Arthur* so this could be just the beginning. I think we need to schedule a meeting with them and Imogene's people asap, start our publicity machine rolling and do some damage limitation."

"Oh." My mum finally spoke, her frozen expression suddenly thawing into tears. She sat down with a bump, her silk dress rustling around her. "Oh, I… I am sorry Jeremy," she said. Her voice was small and she had two pink spots on her cheeks. "I've embarrassed you terribly."

"But nothing they've written here is true, Mum!" I exclaimed as I finished reading. I wanted to hug her but I couldn't unless I shoved Jeremy aside. "You are very fashionable," I told her. "And you look great for your age and, OK, you're not as beautiful as Carenza Slavchenkov, but you're a normal mum not a supermodel!"

It was then my mum started to properly cry and I got the feeling I had made things worse. She turned her face into Jeremy's shoulder and his arms enclosed her.

"What I meant to say was—" I tried again, but Michael spoke over me impatiently.

"Jeremy, we need to set up that meeting. We have to think about the movie."

"And we will," Jeremy said, his voice low as he held my mother. "But right now, Michael, you need to go."

"I'll call you," Michael said, making a phone shape with his thumb and little finger and holding it to his ear.

"I have no doubt that you will," Jeremy said heavily.

Mum was crying and Jeremy was hugging her and telling her he was so sorry that knowing him had put her in this position, and they seemed as if they were in their own separate world, a world I didn't have a passport to. So I thought it was probably best if I just got out of the way for a while.

As I picked up the offending magazine and took it into the kitchen where Augusto was making sushi for lunch, I realised that David was scampering after me.

"Feeling left out too?" I asked the dog.

Of course he didn't answer, but as his tiny nails clicked on the floor tiles I let myself think it was me he wanted to be with and not the scraps he might get in the kitchen. Because just at that moment I needed a pal and even a rat dog was better than nothing.

"That's pretty bad," Augusto said when I showed him the magazine. "These journalists, they don't think about anyone's feelings. They don't care as long as they've got something to write in their nasty little rags."

"And it's not fair," I said. "Poor Mum, she's really hurt. I know what it feels like to hear that people think you're ugly. But she's not. She's just mum-looking, that's all!"

"Which is a very beautiful way to look," Augusto said.

"I tried to cheer her up, but I think I just made it worse," I added miserably. "I don't know what to say to her."

"Just tell her that you love her," Augusto said. "Telling someone that can never make them feel worse."

"S'pose," I said, looking towards the other room where Jeremy was probably doing exactly that. I wasn't exactly jealous, but how could I tell Mum anything if she was always with him? I realised that I hadn't spent any time on my own with her all holiday and, even more amazingly, I realised that I missed doing that. Even though usually it meant me doing the washing-up while she dried, or folding while she ironed, I liked talking things over with her. We hadn't done that in ages.

"And that other stuff isn't so good either," Augusto said, wielding a large and very sharp knife as he thinly sliced some ginger. I wrinkled up my nose. I really didn't like the idea of raw fish for lunch.

"What other stuff?" I asked him, eyeing some bright orange, globular fish roe suspiciously.

"About the movie, *your* movie! They are bad-mouthing the film before it even opens and that can't be good."

"What?" I said. I picked up the magazine and read the piece again.

"Oh," I said heavily. I had been too busy being cross to notice it before. "But it can't be that bad, can it? A couple of nasty comments in one magazine?"

Augusto raised an eyebrow. "If they want to, the press can sink a great film and make a success out of a real turkey."

He offered me a salmony-looking thing and I backed away hastily. To my surprise David jumped up on to my lap, digging his bony little feet into my thighs, and looked hard at Augusto as if to say he'd try anything I wouldn't. Augusto threw him a scrap of fish which he caught deftly between his teeth and then waited hopefully for more. I stroked his bony back, which was not nearly as soft as Everest's, but his warmth on my lap was still quite comforting.

"But why? Why would they want to do that?" I asked, shaking my head.

"Because their only concern is to sell magazines and if they were always lovely to everyone then nobody would buy any. It's sad but true, Ruby. It's the meanness and the cruelty that sells copies. The A-list actress who looks fat in a dress, the latest marriage to fail after only six months, the illustrious careers that tumble and fall over one 'bad' film."

"But that wouldn't happen to Jeremy," I said. "He's a British institution, even if he is my mum's boyfriend. Or to Imogene Grant. Imogene is real star."

"No, it wouldn't happen to Jeremy," Augusto agreed. "Or Miss Grant, but for other actors, younger actors, maybe who were just starting out – well it could mean their career is ended before it even really began."

"Oh," I said, eyes wide. "Well, that would be terrible. I mean, you spend all that time working hard on a—" I stopped talking and looked at Augusto. "Like *me*, you mean?" I asked, feeling sick in the pit of my stomach.

"Don't worry, Ruby," Augusto said. "If anyone can turn things around it's Jeremy and, like you say, it's only a few comments in one magazine. It might be nothing to worry about at all." He smiled his big warm smile at me, but I thought about the conversation that Micheal had just had with Jeremy and I didn't feel very much better.

"I can see by the look on your face that you aren't really looking forward to my sushi," Augusto said sympathetically. "Anything else I can whip you up for lunch?"

"A plane ticket home?" I asked him miserably. "I think I'm finished in Hollywood."

"Don't be silly," Augusto told me. "You haven't even begun yet."

Suddenly David leapt up and, putting his paws on my shoulder, licked my neck.

"Look, even David's trying to make you feel better," Augusto said with a chuckle. "You're honoured that dog likes you."

"Either that," I said, squirming "or he wants to eat me."

When I went back to tell Mum and Jeremy the sushi was ready, Mum seemed happier and brighter, even though her face was still smudged with tears.

"You're sure that's what you want?" Jeremy was asking her as I approached. He had one hand on each shoulder as he looked into her eyes. "Because I want you to know that I think you are utterly perfect exactly the way you are."

I nearly turned round and walked back out the room to simultaneously die of embarrassment and throw up. But my curiosity won out and I stood my ground. I wanted to know what it was that Mum was absolutely sure about.

"I am," Mum said with a brave little smile. "And besides, if I am going to be with you, then I have to be prepared for this kind of attention."

At that point I realised that Jeremy was probably going to kiss my mum in front of me, possibly with *tongues* and everything. I like to think that I've been quite cool about things like my dad's so-called girlfriend and my mum's megastar man, but witnessing *that* would be a step too far.

"A-*hem*!" I coughed loudly enough to make the pair jump apart and had to suppress a smirk. "The raw fish thing is served, but I'm having a cheese toastie because frankly it looks disgusting to me."

Jeremy and Mum smiled indulgently at me and as we walked back to the kitchen Jeremy patted me on the back and said, "Are you sure, Ruby? It's good to broaden your horizons, you know, take a chance every now and then."

"Yes," I agreed. "And I want to do that, but I don't want to eat raw fish. Because it's fish and it's raw."

I waited for either one of them to tell me what they had been talking about, but they clearly weren't going to. "So?" I asked as we sat down at the table and I saw my mum looking rather fondly at my cheese toastie. "What have you two decided?"

"Oh!" Mum said, looking at Jeremy in a secretive way I didn't like at all, like I was an outsider. "Nothing much. We were just planning what to do after New Year. Jeremy says we've got to make the most of our time left here. I am going to a day spa and salon to have a few treatments, get my hair and nails done, that sort of thing…"

"Really?" I said, thinking a few highlights and some false nails might make her feel better. "Good idea. Am I coming too? Can I go blonde, *please*, Mum? I am nearly fourteen."

Jeremy smiled. "No, Ruby, you are coming with *me*. While you were helping Augusto, I phoned Michael. You and I are going into Wide Open Universe Studios. We're going to watch a screening of *The Lost Treasure of King Arthur*, and talk about publicity with Art and Imogene and all the studio people."

"Are we?" I cheered up. "It will be nice to see Imogene again, and Art – but what about Harry?" Harry McLean was Imogene's leading man, although I never really got to know him very well as he spent a lot of time in his trailer.

"Ah, nooo, I'm afraid not," Jeremy said, looking down at his sushi. "He's not very well at the moment. He's in a special type of hospital getting better."

"Better from what?" I asked him.

"Well – let's just say that too much of anything is bad for you, Ruby," Jeremy told me with a shrug.

"Even sushi?" I asked him, annoyed not only that he wouldn't tell me, but that he wouldn't tell me in such a smug way. After all, I'd had plenty of experience with celebrity health problems before. Brett Summers, my old TV mum, was always in and out of clinics because of her intolerance to alcohol, and Imogene Grant had told me herself about the eating disorder that had nearly killed her. And even though she isn't quite a celebrity yet, even my best friend Nydia had collapsed and banged her head badly because she'd stopped eating to try and make herself thin. I knew what the pressures of fame could do to a person. I didn't need Jeremy to keep it from me.

"Anyway," Jeremy went on, smiling at me like I was next door's toddler, "perhaps if there is time we might be able to show you the set of my new film. The actors are all still on break, but you'll enjoy seeing the sets, won't you?"

I should have been over the moon. I should have been cart-wheeling in excitement, but nobody, except possibly David, seemed to have noticed how the events of that morning, the column in *People's Choice Magazine* and its sly digs at *The Lost Treasure of King Arthur*, might affect *me*. All of that, topped off with Jeremy and Mum kissing, and his smug, smiling ways had put me in a sulk.

"Whatever," I said quite rudely, pushing my plate away so that it skidded across the polished granite surface. "So for the rest of today I can do what I like, right?"

They nodded, Mum with her thin lips pressed together and a "I'll talk to you later, young lady" look on her face.

"Can I phone Dad then?" I asked.

"Of course you can, Ruby," Jeremy answered. "Use the phone in your room if you want to be private."

"I was going to anyway," I said, knowing I sounded childish, but not quite able to stop myself. "And then I'm going to see if I have any e-mails and I might have a swim after and then I'll..." I looked around the room for something else to list. "I'll take David for a walk. I expect I'll be busy until dinner, so don't worry about me – if you were going to anyway, which I doubt. Oh, and Happy New Year!"

And then I flounced. I flounced out of the kitchen and up the stairs and (because I was too busy flouncing with my chin in the air) I flounced into the laundry cupboard and slammed its door shut. Hoping they hadn't realised, I waited for a moment or two and then ran down the hall to where my room really was and slammed that door too for good measure.

It was a horrible way to behave. Rude and, as my mum would no doubt tell me later, very unattractive. But I couldn't help it. That was the way I felt. I was all churned up and cross, and I suppose a bit jealous and left out, and I didn't like it.

I found the phone next to the bed and the piece of paper Jeremy had written down the international dialling code on for me and dialled Dad's number.

It would be evening back at home, so I was certain that Dad would answer.

I was wrong.

It was Dad's so-called girlfriend who answered.

Hi Ruby

How is it going over there? Sorry I haven't e-mailed sooner. I've been really busy with the new family that have just started on Kensington Heights because I have a lot of scenes with the daughter, a girl our age called Melody Butler. She's playing a character called Lacey St Claire. I spent Christmas Day at my dad's this year which was quite a laugh as my little brother is still really into it and nearly had a heart attack when he saw Dad had got him a bike! And then I spent Boxing Day at my mum's which was OK. I got some good presents. An MP3 player (but not an iPod), some trainers and, wait for it... A Christmas number one! I know it's amazing, isn't it? I can't believe that Liz finally talked me into recording that awful song, but anyway now *Kensington Heights (You take me to...)* is a hit and it was only released the week before Christmas! I don't know what they did to my awful voice, but it sounds all right and loads of people bought it! There is even talk about an album, but I don't know about *that*.

I bet you are seeing loads of celebrities and forgetting about all of us little people! Looking forward to seeing you in a few days.

Danny

PS Nydia did an audition for this part on a new CBBC show called *Totally Busted*.

Chapter Three

At first when I heard a woman's voice I thought I must have the wrong number so I said, "Sorry, I thought this was Frank Parker's number."

But just before I could put the phone down the female voice stopped me. "It is! It is Frank's number. Hello – is that Ruby? I'm Denise."

I said nothing for what seemed like a long time.

"Denise," the voice on the other end of the phone said again, sounding totally natural and even quite amused. "Your father's so-called girlfriend."

I felt my cheeks burning pink and thanked my lucky stars that she couldn't see me. It was one thing to have a fairly rude nickname for a person behind their backs, but it was another thing entirely to realise that the person knew about it. I couldn't believe my dad had told her, especially when she was now supposed to be his *ex* so-called girlfriend. I couldn't work out why she was there at all.

"The thing is," I said, "I'm calling from America and it

is probably costing my mum's so-called boyfriend a lot of money, so can I talk to Dad, please?"

Denise laughed. "I like you, Ruby," she said. "Very direct."

"You haven't even met me," I said. At least my dad hadn't forced that particular ordeal on me. Yet. Maybe by half term I'd find myself on a wet and windy beach in Brighton with so-called Denise. Well, if she liked direct, I'd give her direct.

"I thought you and Dad had split up?" I said. I would never normally ask an adult that kind of question in that kind of way, but as she was so far away it didn't quite seem real.

Denise laughed again. "Oh no, dear, we just had a misunderstanding. It's all cleared up now."

"Can you put Dad on, please?" I asked.

"Can't, love. He's popped out to the shop. He'll be back in a few minutes. We could chat while we wait if you like. I'm sure Jeremy Fort can afford it." Denise laughed. I did not. And I couldn't actually believe what came out of my mouth next.

"Yes, he can afford it," I said, sounding exactly like I thought Anne-Marie did when she was giving someone the brush off. "But I don't want to talk to you."

I put down the phone and for about fifteen seconds I felt quite pleased with myself. And then I remembered that I phoned Dad to try and make up with him, and that being rude to his ex- or un-ex-so-called girlfriend was not the best way to go about it.

I didn't know what was wrong with me. OK, I was feeling a bit fed up about Mum and Jeremy, and worried about what *People's Choice Magazine* said about the film (and my mum). But I wasn't acting like me at all. I'm not rude to people and I don't talk back, and I never put the phone down on someone after insulting them because I'm me, Ruby Parker – really bad at rebelling. Maybe my mum was right to be worried about me keeping my feet on the ground because suddenly I felt untethered, as if I was careering off in all directions like a popped balloon. I didn't like it, but I didn't know how to stop it.

I thought about picking up the phone again and saying sorry to Denise, but I couldn't bring myself to do it. I knew that the next time I spoke to or saw Dad I was going to be in really big trouble with him. I half expected him to call here and tell my mum how dreadful I'd been. So I decided not to phone back. I'd face the music when I saw him and we could make up then, because hopefully by then I'd be me again.

That's when I checked my e-mails on the laptop in my room. There was only one e-mail in my inbox and I was glad to see it was from Danny. When I saw his name there my heart skipped a beat and I smiled to myself.

At least I could rely on Danny. He was a good friend and even though we'd nearly split up that time he thought that I was in love with Sean Rivers we had stuck together.

I couldn't believe his news! I knew that Liz Hornby, the producer, had finally persuaded Danny to record the *Kensington Heights* theme tune as a song because Nydia and I went along with him to the studio when he made it.

Me and Nydia had laughed all day because as lovely as Danny is, and as good-looking, he really can't sing at all. He did about a million takes and each one seemed worse than the last. Even Danny was laughing about it and said that the only hope of saving his career was if the record was so bad it sank without anybody ever hearing it.

Well, it looks like that didn't happen. It occurred to me that maybe Danny was joking, so I logged on to the UK Top 40. Sure enough there it was in black and white: 1. Danny Harvey *Kensington Heights* (*You take me to...*).

I was going out with a proper pop star (or quite possibly a proper one-hit wonder, but anyway, I didn't care). I was proud of him.

Suddenly, I wanted to speak to Danny really badly and I looked at the phone. Mum and Jeremy had said I could call Dad. They hadn't exactly said I couldn't call anybody else, but then again they hadn't definitely said I could call who I liked and Mum was strict about our bill at home (including my mobile) so I was fairly sure she wouldn't approve.

I supposed I could go downstairs and ask permission to call Danny, but that would mean finding them, possibly interrupting them mid tongue-type kissing and then having to say sorry and be nice, something I was having trouble doing just now. Anyway, feeling uncharacteristically rebellious once again, I decided that, as Dad's so-called and apparently not ex-girlfriend had said, Jeremy could afford it.

"You're a genius," I said as soon as I heard Danny's voice.

"Oh, Rube!" he said a little hesitantly as if caught off guard. "Hiya! What a nice surprise!" I was happy at how pleased to hear from me he sounded. "It's mad, isn't it? My rubbish record at number one! I'll never have any rock credibility ever again."

"You never did anyway," I laughed. "But seriously, Danny – that's amazing. Wait till you get back to school. Michael Henderson is going to *die* with jealousy."

"I think he already has over Anne-Marie and Sean." Danny paused. "So how was your Christmas?" he asked.

"Weird," I said. "Jeremy and Mum are like the geriatric version of Anne-Marie and Sean, all gooey and ooey and *I love you, I love you, I love you!*"

"Seriously?" Danny said, chuckling.

"Well, I haven't actually heard them *say* the 'I love you' thing, but I wouldn't be surprised. The ooey and gooey stuff is a horrific fact I have to live with on a daily basis. But I suppose Mum needed it today. The paparazzi took a photo of her and it got printed in this horrible magazine that said horrible things about her."

"That's dreadful, Ruby," Danny said. "Is she OK?"

"The thing is I don't know. She seems all right, but she hasn't really talked to me about it. Jeremy's looked after her and tomorrow she's going to get her hair and nails done. She'll be OK," I said. "Back to normal Mum settings soon."

Danny laughed. "So, Ruby Parker, how's America? Is it as exciting and as glam as you thought it would be?"

I thought about the article in *People's Choice Magazine*.

"It *is*, but it's also much more like being in a foreign country than I thought it would be. No, scrap that, it's like being on another planet. Even Jeremy's different here – he's even got a celebrity dog!" I said, making Danny laugh as I told him about my first meeting with David. His laugh made my tummy tense.

"I miss you," I mumbled before I knew what I'd said.

"When are you back?" Danny asked me, without telling me he missed me too.

"About a week. We fly home on January 6th," I told him. "I'm actually looking forward to going back to school."

"Me too," Danny said, and I thought I could hear a smile in his voice. "OK then, Ruby, I'll see you in a week."

I knew he was being all cool and offhand because once I had told him that he carried on like Romeo out of *Romeo and Juliet*, all overdramatic and far too serious. He had taken that information to heart. A little bit too close to heart, I sometimes felt, especially now when I felt so lonely and he seemed so far away.

"I'll see you then," I said, wanting to say more but not knowing how to.

"*Ciao*, baby," Danny said in an appalling Italian accent and then he was gone.

I felt better and worse when I put the phone down. Better because talking to Danny had cheered me up, but worse because I couldn't just go round to his house to watch TV, or meet him at the café on the corner for hot chocolate, or try to outrun screaming mobs of ten-year-olds with him. And I missed that.

Just then I heard a strange scraping and scratching outside my room, and a high-pitched whimper. I got up and opened the door. David trotted in and with some effort scrambled up on to my bed, and after turning three clockwise circles, he curled up in a tiny ball, his nose on his paws, and looked at me.

"I haven't got any food in here," I told him. "And I've put all of my shoes out of your reach since the trainer incident so you might as well go."

But David didn't move an inch. As I gingerly sat back down on the bed I expected him to attack me at any moment, but he didn't. All he did was get up to move closer to me, turn in three clockwise circles again and then curl up into another little ball, only this time with his tiny body pressed right against mine.

I didn't know why David the dog had decided to stop trying to eat me and my possessions and start trying to be my friend, but just at that moment I was really happy that he had.

David and I spent the rest of the afternoon exactly as I said I would. We wandered about the garden and I threw a tennis ball for him which he would chase, but which was too big for him to get his jaws around and bring back, so I ended up throwing it and fetching with David at my heels. Then I went for a swim in the pool while David stood at the edge, his little legs trembling. Once I'd dried off, we walked down Jeremy's long, tree-lined drive and peeped out between the wrought-iron railings of his security gates. The sweep of the road was completely silent, and with the view shrouded by trees, I thought that I could be anywhere in the world.

David could easily have slipped out between the railings, but he seemed quite content to stay where he was.

"You're small and rather annoying," I said to him. "But I can't imagine how anybody could ever throw you out on to the street. It must have been horrible for you feeling so alone and left out in the cold, even though it's mainly hot here. You're lucky someone kind like Jeremy found you and took you in."

On impulse I picked David up and carried him back to the house. After all, everyone deserves a helping hand now and again. And the heat of his little body against mine took my mind off what was really worrying me.

Tomorrow was the day that I would really find out what this town was about. Tomorrow would be crunch time for Ruby Parker, film actress.

It was when David and I came down to find food that Mum finally accosted me. "I hope you know how ashamed I am of you, young lady," she said, stopping at the foot of the stairs and crossing her arms. I looked at her in her jeans and T-shirt and I realised what was wrong – no sparkly pink silk dress.

"Aren't you getting ready? You'll be late for the Zeta-Jones-Douglas's," I said.

Mum shook her head. "There is no way I can go to something like that when I look like this," she gestured at herself. "Everyone will have seen that magazine and if they don't laugh in my face, they will behind my back. No, I need to make a few adjustments before my next public appearance."

"You don't, Mum," I said. "Honestly. You look lovely and Jeremy fell for you, not some glossy plastic-looking model."

Mum's smile softened her face but I could see she was determined to tell me off. "Stop trying to change the subject," she said firmly.

"What subject?" I asked, trying my best to look innocent. "Hey look, me and David have made friends! I'm thinking of changing his name to Fido. That way he might not be embarrassed to hang out with the other dogs on the street."

"Ruby." Mum tried her best not to smile, forcing a frown that was not nearly as scary as it should be. "You were very rude to Jeremy earlier, to someone who I thought you liked and respected as a friend. Jeremy has been very generous and kind to you."

"I know," I said, dropping my chin. "And I'm sorry, Mum, I really am. It's just that since we got here—"

"After all, Ruby, if you want to be treated like an adult you have to act like one," Mum went on, clearly intent on getting all of her best lines into my lecture before she'd let me go. "It's unattractive to see a girl of your age sulking and pouting like a three-year-old. I have not brought you up to be a prima donna and if I thought that for one minute experiencing all this is going to change you then—"

"It's not me who's changing," I said. "I mean, it is me a bit. I know I've not been myself lately. But it's because everything else is changing. You're changing, Mum. I'm not saying it's a bad thing. I like to see you so happy – well, mostly happy. It's just that you and Jeremy are always together and I feel... out of it and that made me sulk and be rude. I'm sorry."

My mum looked at me for a moment and then hugged me very tightly so that my ribs ached, and David wriggled out of my arms and scampered off to safety.

"Oh, Ruby, I'm sorry," she said. "I should have realised. It must be hard for you to see me with someone apart from your dad."

"It is a bit," I said. "I *do* like Jeremy, I really do, but I like him better at home in our house where he's the guest and he doesn't seem so..."

"So what?" Mum asked me, keeping her voice level.

"Smug," I said with a shrug. To my relief Mum laughed before making her face go serious again.

"Jeremy is not smug, and even if he was, that would be no excuse for rudeness, young lady. Jeremy really cares for you and he's told me he thinks that you have real talent, talent that could go all the way." I saw a glint of something in Mum's eyes then, as if for the first time she was really excited instead of just anxious about what the future might hold for me. "Look at what he's doing for you tomorrow," she went on. "Taking you to the studio, introducing you to a lot of important people – people who could really make your career."

"I know. And that's exciting but... well, I don't know, Mum. Sometimes I think..." I trailed off.

"What?" Mum asked, but I didn't want to say the thought that had popped into my head because it was the first time I had ever had it, and if it had taken me by surprise, then it certainly would my mum.

"Oh, nothing," I said. "I'm tired and in a muddle."

"OK, Rubes," Mum said and she ruffled my hair exactly the way she knows I hate and kissed me on the forehead. "Well, at least you can stay up with and see the new year in with us. We've got hot chocolate all round."

"That sounds nice," I said. "Although I might not make it to midnight after all."

Mum put her arm around me as we walked together to find Jeremy and the hot chocolate.

"You know what, Ruby," my mum said. "I think this New Year is going to be the most amazing one yet.

It's Your Life!

The magazine for girls that have really got it going on

WHAT MAKES A HOT CHICK HOT?

Top five tips on how to be fabulous and fiery like some of our favourite teen stars.

1 BE FABULOUS! Take actress Adrienne Charles who plays Natalie Green, the meanest girl in hit TV series *Hollywood High*. Adrienne's character might be cruel, unkind, unscrupulous and unhinged, but in real life this girl is a sweetie. She always knows just what fabulous thing to wear and when to wear it, and Adrienne's work with animal welfare charities shows us all her fabulous true colours.

2 BE THE BEST! While we're talking about *Hollywood High*, how about Nadine Navarro? There's a girl we can all take a tip from. Nadine might play feisty and fun cheerleading heroine Sabrina Silkwood in the show, but in real life she still plays competitive soccer to the highest standard for her school and is tipped to be picked as one of the national team's under-eighteen side. You rock, Nadine!

3 NEVER GIVE UP! Sometimes life is hard. Just look at new-to-the-big-screen actress Sunny Dale. Sunny couldn't have had a worse start to life, losing both her parents in a tragic accident when she was only three years old. Growing up poor was hard for Sunny, but she overcame it all with her strength and determination to follow her dream. And *It's Your Life!* has heard that Sunny is tipped to be at the top after her amazing performance in the new Brit flick *A Very English Affair*, due to hit our screens later this year. Way to go nailing that British accent, Sunny!

4 BE FIERCE! You know it's true, it doesn't matter what sort of day you are having as long as you give it fierce attitude. Take this month's cover girl, Samantha Haven. Her heart must have been broken when her rumored boyfriend, super-hot Sean Rivers, disappeared last year, announcing his retirement from the movie industry. But do you see a miserable girl before you? No, you see a fabulous, fierce lady giving life her very best shot!

5 THINK BIG! You've seen all of the great girls we've featured in this week's issue of *It's Your Life!* None of them ever had small dreams. They wanted to get to the top from the very start, and through hard work and talent they are making it. And you can make it too, in any walk of life you choose, as a surgeon, an explorer or maybe even an actress too. But you have to think big and dream big and never let those dreams go!

Chapter Four

I picked up a copy of *It's Your Life!* on the way to the studio with Jeremy when he asked his driver to stop on the corner so he could get a copy of *The Times* from a newsstand. Not the *LA Times*, but the London *Times*. Jeremy told me he misses it when he's not living in Britain. He likes the rain, the rude and miserable people and the buildings. I looked out of the window with my big sunglasses at the faultless blue sky and I wondered what on earth he was going on about.

I wondered who all these actresses they were talking about were. I hadn't seen an episode of *Hollywood High* although before we left home Channel 4 were trailing it as coming up on UK TV in the spring. I looked at the pictures of the featured actresses. All were about my age. Each one looked amazingly glossy. I mean their hair, their lips, their skin, their teeth, their nails and even their clothes seemed to shine. It was a sort of perfect finish that most TV actors, especially teens, just don't have in Britain (except some on *Hollyoaks*, maybe).

And then I read the bit about Sunny Dale. Jeremy was acting in a film with her and he had never even told me. When I asked him what *A Very English Affair* was about, he said it was really just about old people's love lives. Not a mention of Sunny or any part in the film for a thirteen-year-old British girl that perhaps the daughter of his girlfriend could have at least auditioned for.

"So what's this Sunny Dale like then?" I asked him. "Apart from having a name that makes her sound like a brand of yoghurt."

Jeremy looked up from his paper and thought for a moment.

"Sunny? Well, I can't say I *know* her. I only have a few scenes with her. But she struck me as a very determined young lady. She used to live on a trailer park, you know, but now she and her aunt live in a great big place not far from mine. Funnily enough, her career did start out with advertising dairy products."

"I thought you were supposed to name stuff after actresses, not the actresses after stuff," I said sarcastically.

There she was again, that Ruby who was not Ruby, being really quite jealous and rude about a girl for no good reason.

"Well, she's a big name in TV over here and everyone relates to her story. And she's a really hard worker."

"Oh," I said, feeling rather stupid.

Jeremy smiled at me over the top of his reading glasses. "It's all been a bit of a whirlwind, hasn't it?" he said. "I hope that your mum being with me doesn't make you unhappy, Ruby?"

I shook my head. "It doesn't. It's not you, Jeremy, although it is kind of odd seeing someone as famous as you hanging out with my mother. I'm not even unhappy. It just takes a bit of getting used to I suppose, all of this..." I gestured at the cream-leather interior of his chauffeur-driven Rolls Royce. "And I'm sorry for how I've been acting."

"Don't be sorry," Jeremy said. "Be happy. You only have a few days left here, Ruby, so make the most of them, OK? Your life will be back to normal before you know it."

I showed Jeremy the photos in the magazine, of Sunny Dale and the rest. "I'm glad it will be because I'll never look like that," I said. "They are so polished and perfect and I'm..." I looked down at myself in my white jeans that had a bit of breakfast on them and my pink cardigan that had the buttons done up all wrong. "I'm me," I said with a shrug.

Jeremy smiled and shook his head. "Trust me, Ruby, none of those girls look like that either, not in normal life.

Magazines like to do two things: find photos of normal-looking people and make them look terrible, as you and your mum both unfortunately know, or they airbrush celebrities until they become the media's version of perfect, with no flaws or extra weight. And as for TV and film, well, *you* know, Ruby – it's all about lighting and make-up."

I thought about Brett Summers, my former TV mother. It was true that while I was working on *Kensington Heights* with her, it did always take much longer to light her sets and do her make-up then anyone else. And whenever she appeared on the front of the TV guide she did always look about ten years younger.

Suddenly, the car slowed down and I looked out of the window. We had stopped at the security gate of Wide Open Universe Studios. It looked, from the outside at least, like a giant whitewashed Arabian castle, with a line of palm trees growing along the perimeter.

"From the 1930s to the late 1960s this place was the hub of the movie world, literally the centre of the film universe," Jeremy told me as we were driven slowly into the complex. "Back then it was the most powerful studio in the world. It owned all the big stars and paid them a regular wage. They used to make hundreds of films here every year. It's not like that now. Studios have to be very careful about which projects they pick to back. They are always looking for the next big thing. They always need to see a return on their investment. It's a tighter, more difficult industry to break into now than it has ever been, Ruby. That's why, if this is what you really want, you have to grasp every chance that comes your way because if you let even one pass you by, it might be the moment that could have changed everything."

"Dream big and never let those dreams go," I said under my breath, quoting *It's Your Life!*. That's what those other girls did; Adrienne Charles and Sunny Dale and the rest. The question was – could I do the same?

Jeremy's car slowed down and came to a halt outside another ornate white building.

"This is where we are going for the screening," Jeremy said. "And then to talk to Art and the others. Are you excited yet? This is the first time you'll have seen yourself on film since the rushes back in London, isn't it? And now it will have all the proper effects in place and the real score. It should be quite something."

"I *am* excited," I said as I climbed out of the car and looked up at the building. "And I'm scared too. What if I'm rubbish?"

But Jeremy didn't answer me.

We saw Art Dubrovnik first, in the foyer of the

screening room, deep in discussion with a very large, tall and quite wide man in a pale blue suit.

"Ruby!" Art said and gave me a big friendly hug. As Art and Jeremy shook hands and exchanged greetings, Imogene arrived with her PA, Clarice, and a few other people I didn't know, but who I imagined were publicists and agents, a proper Hollywood entourage.

"Hey you!" Imogene said, beaming. She hugged me and kissed me on both cheeks, proper slightly sticky lip-glossy kisses, not the "Mwah! Mwah!" air kisses that actresses often exchange.

"Let me look at you." Imogene held me by the shoulders and looked me up and down. "You look fabulous. How are you feeling – are you excited? Are you nervous?"

I laughed, made giddy by the whirlwind that was Imogene Grant. It was nice that she was so pleased to see me, but there was something else about her too. She was glowing with joy.

"You look lovely. And really, *really* happy. Have you found the secret to a perfect cheese and salad sandwich?" I asked her, joking about the lunches we used to share on the set of *The Lost Treasure of King Arthur*.

Imogene flashed me a grin and then drew me aside so that we stood just out of earshot of the gathering crowd of people. "Can you keep a secret?" she asked.

I nodded excitedly as Imogene looked around to check for eavesdroppers and then took a long silver chain out from under her white cotton shirt. Dangling on it like a pendant was a ring set with the biggest diamond I had ever seen. (And, just recently, I had seen quite a lot of diamonds one way or another.)

"I'm engaged," she told me in a giggly whisper. "But it's top secret. You mustn't tell anyone or the paparazzi will be all over me like flies and it will be spoiled. I know they'll get hold of the story eventually, but not yet, not until I'm ready. For now this is just my secret treasure to keep locked away in here."

She patted her chest and I was wondering how she kept anything locked in there when I realised she meant her heart.

"Who to?" I asked her, keeping my voice low and looking round. Imogene's smile was radiant as she leant forward and whispered a name in my ear.

"WOW!" I said. "I didn't even know you were going out with him!"

Imogene laughed. "That, Ruby," she said, "was the point. It's extremely hard keeping stuff like this a secret so, please, not word. Promise?"

"I promise," I said solemnly. She slipped the ring she could not wear back under her top and we went back to the throng that was waiting to see the screening.

Michael White had arrived and a few other people that Jeremy knew, including the large man in the pale blue suit who everybody seemed to gather around, including Art. The last to arrive was Lisa Wells, who was talking on the phone as she swept into the viewing room, smiling and winking at me as she went past.

"OK, guys!" Art called out as we filed into the viewing room, which was a bit like a miniature cinema. "Take your seats. Sit back and enjoy."

I listened as the swell of the opening music played over the titles of the film and then I leant back in my seat and held my breath.

Preview Report compiled by Lisa Wells for Art Dubrovnik
The Lost Treasure of King Arthur
Directed by Art Dubrovnik
Starring Imogene Grant, Jeremy Fort, Harry Mclean and Sean Rivers
Introducing Ruby Parker

- Test audiences in theaters scored the film quite highly with an overall mark of **8/10**

- For Thrilling Action they gave it an overall score of **9/10**
- For Plot they gave it an overall score of **7/10**
- 73% said that the plot was sometimes hard to follow
- For actors' performances they gave it an overall score of **7/10**
- 48% would go and see it for Imogene Grant, regardless
- 94% enjoyed her performance
- 89% enjoyed Jeremy Fort in the role of Professor Darkly
- 72% were disappointed by Harry McLean, but we have to take into consideration his recent fall in popularity
- 68% came purely for Sean Rivers in case it was his last film. This alone should ensure a healthy box-office turnover
- 78% of the test audiences thought that the young actress Ruby Parker made an impressive debut
- As an Art Dubrovnik film they scored it **6/10**
- 54% stated they preferred Mr Dubrovnik's

less commercial work. But when asked
again to score the film purely on
entertainment and enjoyment factor the
score went up to **8/10**

These scores were compiled from results
taken from fifty screenings shown
nationwide and represent the views of
approximately 5000 people over a wide
demographic.

As the credits rolled I leapt out of my seat and applauded
wildly. It took me a minute or two to realise I was the
only one doing it.

"Sorry," I said, feeling myself blush. "It's not cool to
applaud yourself, is it?"

Imogene laughed and stood up to join me.
"Sometimes it is," she said, starting to clap. Gradually,
everyone else in the room joined in and we all gave
ourselves a standing ovation. Maybe it was a bit like
"blowing your own trumpet" as my granny would say,
but I thought that considering I had just seen myself for
the first time in a proper film I could be let off.

I sat down again as the adults talked. I couldn't quite

believe what I had seen. It was me, but not me. At first, while I was watching, all I could think of was what had happened on the day when that particular scene had been shot, or spotting that I had been wearing costume number four. (I had worn the same school uniform for most of the filming, except that there were thirty-two different versions, each one in a worse state of repair than the last depending on where I was in the story.) Or I found myself thinking that my face looked a bit funny from that camera angle, especially when it was blown up a gazillion times, so you could see all the pores on my nose.

But then I finally saw the shot of my character Polly Harris as she dangled off what now really looked like a real precipice with a fatal drop below. I saw Polly leap into midair and disappear into the black void to her certain death. From that minute on I wasn't watching me any more. I was watching the film. And perhaps I am biased, but I thought it was pretty good.

The lights went up and as we sat back down in our seats Lisa handed out sheets of A4 paper. As I read it took a while for me to understand what it was because I had no idea that reports like this even existed.

"Well, Art," the big man in the blue suit who got to sit in the front row said, "I think that has a chance of being a box-office winner, I really do. Despite everything."

"Thanks, Jim," Art said.

"It's a little long," the man called Jim said, and I held my breath, certain that Art would lose his temper at such an offensive comment. Art was a perfectionist; he never got anything wrong.

But all Art did was nod, adding mildly, "I think I can safely trim about ten minutes off and also improve the audience's understanding of the plot."

"And that's why we pay you what we do, Art. And it seems that the audience will love it," Jim said, gesturing at the piece of paper in his hand, "if they ever go and see it."

"But why wouldn't they?" I asked, conscious a second or two later that as a thirteen-year-old and the least important person here, I probably shouldn't be saying anything. The man in the pale blue suit called Jim twisted in his seat to look at me.

"Miss Parker," he said, offering me a plump hand. "Pleased to meet you, I don't think you and I have been formally introduced. I'm Jim Honeycutt, head of Wide Open Universe."

"Oh," I replied, awestruck. "Oh gosh, I'm sorry. I didn't realise. I shouldn't have said anything..."

"On the contrary, Miss Parker," Mr Honeycutt said. "It's a question that needs to be addressed even if I think that by now most of us know the answer..."

"I don't," I said before I could stop myself.

"Quite." Jim Honeycutt looked very serious. "The critics hate it. Or should I say, they want to hate it. Nobody wanted Art to do anything different. They feel he has betrayed his art-house roots to make money…"

"That's not true," Art said crossly. "All I wanted to do was make a quality entertainment picture, to show all those other bozos out there how to do it…"

"I know, Art, I know," Jim soothed him with a wave of his giant hands. "And a lot of people are angry about Harry Mclean. And, most significantly some people, namely one Mr Pat Rivers, is blaming this film for pushing his cash pot of a son into what he alleges is a nervous breakdown and ruining his career."

"Well, that's just rubbish," I said. "Sean is incredibly happy at the moment, not nervous or broken down at all."

"Might have to quote you on that, Ruby," Lisa said, making a note on her clipboard.

"But you can't," I replied. "I promised Sean I wouldn't talk about him to anyone. He wants to be out of the spotlight."

"Well, we'll see," Jim said as if he hadn't completely understood me. "We might need that young man and he did sign a contract with publicity obligations. And although the nation loves Imogene, she's been at the top for a long time now. It could be the critics are just waiting for a chance to knock her down."

"But that's horrid," I said in a small voice. "And it's not true; it's a good film and Imogene is the best thing in it."

"That might be so, Miss Parker," Jim said. "But this business is like a fish pond full of sharks. If you want to survive in it, you've got to be a shark too."

Lisa Wells stood up and walked to the front of the small theatre. "There's no need to panic," she told everyone. "We all know that films can be a huge success without critical or press approval. Just look at last year's biggest grossing movie, *Giant Dinosaurs in Manhattan*. *No one* liked it; *everybody* went to see it."

"And that was a dreadful film," Art said under his breath.

"What we need to do," Michael said, "is get to our audience directly. Everyone needs to do as much TV and radio as possible. Jeremy, it's late notice but I've got you on the Carl Vine show tonight. OK?"

Jeremy nodded. "OK. And I can take Ruby on with me."

I looked from Mike to Jeremy and back again. "Pardon?"

"It's a talk show, Ruby," Imogene explained, seeing my confusion. "It's taped 'as live' and is getting very high ratings at the moment. Carl will interview you, make some jokes at your expense, perhaps try to embarrass you a little. All you have to do is charm the studio audience and the people at home, and they will want to go and see our film. It's simple."

"Um, what, me?" I said. "I've never done that kind of TV before. I won't be any good at it. I mean, I'm thirteen. I'm permanently embarrassed. Any more and I might drop dead of fatal mortification."

Everybody laughed and I felt my cheeks grow hot. I hadn't been joking.

"That's a good line," Jim said. "Use it." He lumbered out of his chair. "Well, I gotta go. Make this happen, people."

"I'm going on national TV in America?" I questioned weakly. "But I'm only supposed to be on holiday!"

"It'll be fine," Jeremy said. "He won't pick on you, you're just a kid. I'll be doing most of the talking."

"Don't worry, Ruby." Lisa walked with us as we headed out to the car. "How many girls your age get to make a TV appearance on vacation – that's something to put on your postcards home. I'll send a stylist and make-up artist over to Jeremy's house before you go. They do make-up at the show, but I want us to have control over how you look. Young, fresh and pretty,

OK? And remember the Queen," Lisa added.

"The Queen?"

"The posher your voice, the more they will love you," Lisa replied in such a terrible English accent that I actually laughed.

"Look, it's a breeze," she said. "This is your chance to get to twenty million viewers."

And after that I didn't take in another word.

Chapter Five

I stared at my reflection in the mirror. True to her word Lisa had sent over not one, not two, but three stylists to the house. One for clothes, one for hair and one for make-up. Cary, Simone and Julian.

They went through everything I brought with me and all the things that I got for Christmas.

"Sorry, honey, but none of that stuff will really do," Cary told me. "It's lovely, but for a TV show you need a little less stretch cotton and a little more pizzazz! But don't worry, we've got a rack full of stuff here that's going to look great."

I looked at the pile of cellophane-covered outfits that had been laid out on my bed. A lot of it looked extremely pink. And although I like pink a lot, because after all I *am* a girl, I rarely if ever choose to be dressed head to foot in it – at least, not since I was about seven. I had a terrible feeling that I was about to be propelled in front of twenty million strangers looking nearly as bad as I had in the lemon-yellow bridesmaid's dress I was almost forced to wear to an award ceremony while we were filming *The Lost Treasure of King Arthur*.

"It's just that, well, if I could wear my own clothes I'd feel more like myself and more relaxed and less likely to wet myself."

All three stylists roared with laughter. "You're a funny kid," Julian said. "You should use that line."

I sighed. For some reason everyone thought I was joking when I certainly was not. And then I had an idea. I pulled out my suitcase from under my bed and took out the top that Dad had given me for Christmas. I had packed it away, neatly folded with the tags still on, because I wanted to wear it the next time I saw him. Knowing my track record for spilling stuff that never quite washes out I decided it would be safer not to wear it at all until then.

"What about this?" I said, holding it up against me. "I was saving it, but I really love it and—"

"Oh my God, no, not that tat!" Cary said, plucking the top from my hand and flinging it across the room where it landed in a crumpled heap on the floor.

"Trust us, darling," Simone said. "We're here to make you look better than you'd ever thought possible."

An hour or so later I stood looking at myself in the mirror. It could have been worse I supposed. I didn't look dreadful. I just didn't look like *me*. And clearly David didn't think so either because he started growling at me again. I looked at David and then at my reflection. "I know what you mean," I said.

They had dressed me in baby-pink three-quarter length trousers with a deep pink sequinned belt. And an immaculate white T-shirt with the word ENGLAND inscribed across it in diamante. Then they had brought out a string of pearls and some pearl stud earrings for me to wear.

"Very English, very sophisticated, very Princess DI," Julian told me as he fastened the necklace.

"Yes, but not very teenage girl," I said bleakly and unheard.

"You can keep them if you like," Simone said. "They are fake – we know you've got a track record!"

"Ha ha!" I fake laughed. It seemed nobody except me wanted to forget the time I accidentally stole thousands of pounds worth of diamonds.

They straightened my hair so that it fell in one long smooth curtain over my shoulders and put a deep pink Alice band on me. They called it an Alice band; I thought of it more as a headband that six-year-olds wear. Simone handed me a deep pink handbag with a diamante clasp on it and Cary laid out a pair of low-heeled deep pink pumps for me to slip on. And then Julian did my make-up.

He said he was going to keep it natural, but it seemed like it took an awful lot of make-up to look like I wasn't wearing any. He slicked on what felt like a whole pot of foundation, followed by powder and then a light pink blusher. I had to try and not blink while he poked my eye out with a mascara wand, or twitch while he carefully applied lip liner, before sloshing on a gallon or so of lip gloss.

"There," he'd said, admiring his work. "As fresh as an English daisy."

Interesting, I thought, because I didn't feel fresh as a daisy. I felt quite a lot as if I had recently been dipped in concrete and left out in the sun to set solid.

Julian positioned me in front of a full length mirror and then stepped aside. "Tah-dah!"

Cary and Simone applauded.

I stared at myself, or at least I tried to, because I, always ever so slightly off-centre and scruffy me, wasn't there. This immaculately turned out girl in fake pearl earrings was not me. Her skin looked flawless, her hair as shiny as a pane of glass and her outfit pristine and perfectly preppy.

"We'll be coming with you to the show so we can make sure you stay as lovely all night, so don't you worry," Cary told me, repositioning a strand of hair that wasn't to his liking.

I smiled carefully at the three of them, slightly nervous that my new face would crack and fall off. "Thank you," I said. "The transformation is very... transforming."

"That's our job, darling," Julian said. "Sow's ear into a silk purse. That's why we're the best."

I was trying to work out if I should be insulted when I heard Jeremy calling me.

"Ruby?" His voice rose from below. "Your mother's back from the salon. Come down and see her – you can exchange make overs!"

I knew my mum would never be able to believe how I looked and I was excited to show her. I would have run down the stairs, except it was hard to with a little dog yapping at my heels, threatening to trip me up at any moment. I didn't properly see my mother until I was standing right in front of her. When I did finally focus on her it was a bit of a shock.

"Oh, Ruby, you look wonderful!" she said, in a voice that was not quite her own. "Quite the young lady."

"*Mother, what have you done to yourself?*" I yelled in reply. For a split second David stopped yapping at me. Then, catching sight of my mother, started growling again, this time at her.

First it was her hair. Mum has nice light brown hair, quite thick and wavy that she wears shoulder length, and every now and then has highlights put in it. But now it was properly blonde, a bright shiny gold like the wrappers on chocolate coins. And instead of hanging down like hair is supposed to, because of the laws of gravity and all of that, it swirled outwards and up in big, overblown, hairsprayed curls that made her look about a foot taller.

Then there was her face. The smile lines around her eyes had gone and so had the "you're in big trouble now" line between her brows. Her face looked as smooth as an egg, and as tight and immobile. That was except for her lips. Her normal Mum lips, the lips that kissed me goodnight every night for the last thirteen years, had ballooned out in what I can only describe as fish lips; lips that made her voice sound not quite like her own any more. The effect was made worse still by the bright red lipstick, a colour that clashed horribly with her extremely orange fake tan.

"I thought you were having your nails done!" I exclaimed. "Not... not all this... *stuff*! You don't look like you any more!"

I watched my mum's face fall, or at least I'm pretty sure it would have if it could have moved, and I immediately regretted what I'd said. I hadn't wanted to hurt her – but it was the shock. It was the shock of not seeing her, but this strange cartoon woman.

Before I could apologise, Mum spoke. "Well, Ruby, it might surprise you to learn that what you think isn't really important," she said, making my mouth drop open. "For once I am doing something just for me, something to make me feel good about myself."

"Good?" I heard my voice rise. "You look anything but good. You look *dreadful*, Mum."

"Well, I think you look wonderful," Jeremy said, putting his arm round my mum's shoulders and shooting me a look of pure disapproval. "Apologise to your mother, Ruby. You've been rude and hurtful."

"I've been honest!" I protested automatically. "Look – even David hates it and animals don't lie!"

Julian gasped and Simone shook her head.

"It's OK, Jeremy," Mum said coolly. "My daughter is entitled to her opinion."

"But she is not entitled to shout at you and embarrass you in this way, in front of all these people," Jeremy said firmly. "If she has an opinion, she should learn to express it in a more productive way and not like a playground bully." He fixed his dark eyes on me. "Apologise, Ruby," he said again.

"You're not my father!" I told him, hardly believing what I was saying out loud.

"No," Jeremy said quietly, "but I am your host and this is my house and you will abide by my rules while you are in it. Apologise to your mother."

I looked at my mum. Somehow I had managed to upset her and Jeremy all at once when I had intended to hurt neither one. I just didn't understand what had happened to her in the salon. It was as if she had had a personality transplant along with her other treatments.

I dropped my head, finding it awkward to back down to Jeremy, but knowing that I had to.

"Sorry, Mum," I said. "And sorry, Jeremy. I didn't mean to be so rude. You look great, Mum, just really different. It was a surprise."

"Well then," my mum said with a stiff smile that was a little bit more like her old self, "you'd better come here and give me a hug then."

She had been about to put her arms around me when Julian stepped in between us.

"Sorry, Mrs Parker," he said. "I can't have any tears or mascara staining these clothes until after the show."

TONIGHT WITH CARL VINE
EPISODE 29

AUTOCUE: ROLLING

CARL: GOOD EVENING AND WELCOME TO ANOTHER EDITION OF TONIGHT WITH CARL VINE. **(CUE APPLAUSE)**
WE'VE GOT A GREAT NIGHT LINED UP FOR YOU ALL THIS EVENING! **(CUE CHEERS)** WE'VE GOT CHRISTIAN DANE HERE TO FINALLY TELL US THE TRUTH ABOUT THOSE ALLEGED REVELATIONS IN PEOPLE'S CHOICE MAGAZINE. **(CUE CHEERS AND WHOOPING)** ALSO JOINING US THIS EVENING IS COMEDIAN AND FUNNY GUY PETE PETERSON. **(IMPROV ASIDE: I HATE THAT GUY, HE'S FUNNIER THAN ME)** AND, LADIES AND GENTLEMEN, WE HOPE THAT TWO VERY IMPORTANT LAST-MINUTE GUESTS WILL BE ABLE TO JOIN US TONIGHT **(IMPROV ASIDE: "IF I CAN EVER SHUT PETE UP, THAT IS)** TO TALK TO US ABOUT THEIR LATEST FILM 'THE LOST TREASURE OF KING ARTHUR'. GET READY TO DRINK SOME TEA WITH ME – IT'S LEGENDARY ENGLISH ACTOR JEREMY FORT AND BRITISH NEWCOMER MISS ROSIE PARKER! **(CUE APPLAUSE)**
BUT ANYWAY, BEFORE OUR FIRST GUEST, I WANT TO TELL YOU ABOUT SOMETHING THAT HAPPENED TO ME TODAY. **(CUE COMIC EXPRESSION AND PAUSE FOR LAUGHTER)** AND I PROMISE YOU THIS IS ABSOLUTELY TRUE…

We all waited in one dressing room as we watched the transmission on a TV attached to the wall. Me, Jeremy, Mum, Julian, Cary and Simone, Michael, not to mention David who had scrambled into the car with me, sat on my lap and threatened to bite the fingertips off anyone who tried to remove him. Every now and then Julian would redo my lip gloss and Simone would tweak my hair. And considering it was a fairly small room, there was a very big atmosphere inside it.

After I had apologised, Mum had changed into one of her new designer outfits especially to come and see Jeremy and me on the Carl Vine show. When she came back I had to admit that she still looked different and not like my mum at all, but she did look like a proper Hollywood lady.

"You look great, amazing, Mum," I had said, risking a quick air kiss. "I didn't mean what I said before. It was just the shock and nerves about being on the show."

I had meant it of course. I hated how she looked. But I didn't want to fall out with her now and, anyway, I hoped that whatever had happened to her face would wear off soon.

"I know," Mum said, patting me with an orange hand while Julian looked on, ready to separate us by force if we tried for a hug. "But things and even people have to change, Ruby. Nothing stays the same forever."

I really hoped that was true about her tangerine tan.

We'd been at the studio for a few minutes when Lisa Wells popped her head round the dressing-room door to tell us she was in the audience and would laugh and cheer at all our jokes.

"What do you mean, all our jokes?" I asked. Lisa laughed. Jeremy did not. Mum and I might have made up, but Jeremy it seemed was still angry. He hadn't spoken to me once since we had left the house. I was about to go on TV when I was supposed to be on holiday, in front of twenty million viewers, with a man who thought I was selfish and spoilt. It was a bit of a worry.

Then Carl Vine himself came in. Well, came half in as he couldn't quite fit in the crowded room. "Wow," he said, all grins. "You got the whole royal family in here, don't you? Sorry about the cramped conditions Jeremy, we didn't know till the last minute that you were bringing a bonus guest. We had to give the best dressing room to that talent contest kid. It was in his rider."

Carl reached out to shake my hand. "Hi, Rosie, really pleased to meet you. I hear you are the next big thing."

"Actually..." I was about to correct him about my name but he had already gone.

"He seems nice," my mum said.

"It's all a façade. Underneath he's as tough as steel,"

Cary said. "That's how he got this far so quickly. He takes no prisoners."

"Really," Mum said thoughtfully. (At least I assumed she was being thoughtful. It was hard to tell when her forehead no longer moved.)

Then a woman in a red sweater and headphones with a worried look on her face was the next to try and squeeze in the room.

"Hi, guys," she said. "Look, we're really hopin' to get you guys on tonight, after all who wants to hear Christian Dane whining all night? But Pete Peterson might be harder to get off, even if Carl hates him. I promise you we'll do our best, OK?"

And then she was gone and we heard the band begin to play and Carl was introducing the show.

I felt my stomach plummet down to my toes like brick through custard, with a kerplop. Carl had introduced me as Rosie Parker! He had told twenty million viewers that I was called something else. And then another thought occurred to me.

"What does she mean, she *hopes* we'll be on?" I asked Jeremy.

"It means," Jeremy replied coolly, without taking his eyes off the TV monitor, "that on these shows they are never sure if they'll be able to fit in all the guests. It's recorded as live, but aired at different times across the states depending on the time zone. So to keep it seeming live and fresh, if one guest goes on a bit, they have to bump the last one."

"So we might not go on at all?" I asked him hopefully.

"Possibly not," Jeremy said with an indifferent shrug.

He was talking to me at last, but he was clearly still cross. I held on very tight to David, until he bit my finger hard enough to leave teeth imprints. At least the pain took my mind off the panic and emptiness.

We all watched the monitor as the first guest came on, a recent winner of a TV talent show who had lied about his past in order to win votes. It turned out that he didn't have a dying kid sister at all, but four strapping brothers who were all in good health and planning on forming a boy band. *People's Choice Magazine* found out and now there was a popular campaign to get the title of winner awarded to the runner-up, a girl called Heidi Vance. Carl joked with Christian for a little while and then asked him how he thought he could get away with cheating the American people. And then Christian started crying, not just one or two tears but actual nasty, loud, snotty, red-faced sobbing.

Carl wrapped up the interview in about thirty seconds and as Christian disappeared off the TV screens we heard his sobs growing louder out in the corridor and someone shouting at him. "You idiot! You total idiot, you've blown it now – don't you remember what we rehearsed? That's your career over."

The woman in the red sweater put her head back round the door and rolled her eyes. "Amateurs," she said. "Well, you two will definitely be going on. We might even need you to fill a little time, OK? So be ready for anything."

I'm sure that Pete Peterson's comic routine was very funny, but I didn't hear any of it because I was too busy being frightened to death and multitasking is not one of my best things.

I kept looking at Jeremy and wishing that he would give a smile or a wink or one of those pep talks he's so good at. But he just kept watching the TV, waiting for our cue to go on.

"Jeremy," I said, but he didn't hear me. "Jeremy!" I repeated his name more loudly this time and he looked at me. "Can I have a word outside?"

He nodded and we went out into the corridor, leaving the dressing-room door open slightly so that we could hear the laughter and applause on the TV as well as echoing up and down the corridor around us.

"Please don't be angry with me any more," I pleaded.

Jeremy shook his head. "I'm not angry with you, Ruby."

"Yes you are. You're angry with me because of what I said to Mum before, and to you. I shouldn't have said it."

"No, Ruby you shouldn't have," Jeremy said. He took a step away from the door and lowered his voice. "I... I love your mother and to see her hurt by the one person she most cares about in the world makes me angry."

"Do you really love her?" I asked him in a whisper, eyes wide.

"Yes, I do actually," Jeremy said. "But I haven't told her that yet, OK – so let's keep it between ourselves."

I nodded as I tried to imagine somebody, anybody, but *especially* Jeremy Fort being in love with my mum. It wasn't that I didn't think she was lovable or pretty (without giant fish lips and orange skin) but it was just that she was my mum. I didn't think that anybody ever fell in love with mums.

"And do you really love her new look?" I asked him tentatively. His expression was hard to read.

"I love *her*, Ruby. I love her the way she was when I met her, and if this makes her happy then I'll love her this way too. I think a lot of it has got to do with the pressure she's been under being with me. Things will settle down when you get back to England."

Including her lips I hoped.

"So now will you stop being cross with me and protect me from Carl Vine?" I asked.

Jeremy laughed and his shoulders relaxed. "You don't need protecting from Carl Vine," he reassured me. "He'll need protecting from you!"

I was still getting used to the heat of the lights, the nearness of the audience and Carl's autocue – which seemed to have every little thing he said between guests written on it – to realise that he had introduced me as Rosie Parker *again*. I supposed that maybe the mix-up over my name might be a good thing. If I completely flopped on this show – which I was highly likely to do – then at least it would be Rosie Parker's career that had finished before it had begun and not mine. I wished that the floor manager had let David come out on set with me. Then I'd have been holding on to him and at least I would have known what to do with my hands, but she said they'd banned pets on set ever since the pooping incident. So David was left behind in the dressing room, furiously trying to scratch his way out through the door.

I sat down on the sofa next to Jeremy and hoped

that was all I would have to do until we left. But Carl spoke to me first.

"So Rosie…" he began.

"Actually, it's Ruby," I said with a wobbly voice and a nervous smile.

Carl Vine pulled the corners of his mouth down and looked at the audience which seemed to make them laugh. "Not Rosie actually?" he said in a mock English accent.

"No," I said, making myself sound as posh as possible just as Lisa had told me. "It actually is Ruby – Ruby Parker is my name actually."

The audience laughed again and so did Jeremy, and I thought, well, if it's this easy to make them laugh, I'll be OK.

"Anything else I should know about?" Carl asked, still using his terrible accent. "Any titles? You're not Lady Ruby, or Duchess Parker, or Princess anything?"

"You may call me Miss Parker," I told him and the audience applauded.

"Ruby Parker," Carl placed his hand on his chest, "I am very sorry we got your name wrong. Ed – fire the researcher!"

There was the sound effect of a gunshot offstage and the audience applauded again.

"So, Miss Parker," Carl said with a smile, "what was

it like shooting your first movie role with the legendary Jeremy Fort?"

"Well, it was amazing," I replied, listening to the sound of my voice in my head. "He's such a talented actor and so gifted and he really, really taught me a lot."

Then Carl turned to Jeremy and I listened and smiled and remembered to sit up straight and suck my tummy in as they exchanged jokes and stories. Then Jeremy told Carl about the film, what it was about and who was in it.

"It's a great family film, one everyone can enjoy," he told Carl.

"It's interesting that you say that, Jeremy," Carl said. "That it is a *family* film, because I hear it wasn't all happy families on set."

"That's rubbish," Jeremy said with a relaxed smile.

"What do you have to say about the rumours that Art Dubrovnik worked young Sean Rivers so hard it drove him to a breakdown, forcing him to give up his multimillion-dollar career.

"I'd say—" Jeremy began, but before he could finish I found myself interrupting.

"That's not true," I said.

Carl looked at me and raised an eyebrow at the audience. "I *know* that's not true," I added because it seemed as if they expected me to say more.

"Well, Ruby, I heard that you and Sean had a little romance going on, so I suppose if anybody would know, it would be you!"

"Sean and me didn't have a romance," I said, forgetting my posh accent for a moment. "We were, *are*, good friends. There *was* a photo of us kissing, but it was just a tiny kiss, over in a second, but of course the papers blew it up out of all proportion. And I suppose it didn't help that Sean and I went straight from a film premiere to my friend's birthday party without remembering to give back all these diamonds I had been lent, so that the police came and nearly arrested us. But we weren't going out together at all; it was only a cover to get Sean's dad off of his back because he wanted to go out with my friend Anne-Marie."

There was a shocked gasp from the audience and I got the feeling that perhaps I'd said a little more than I should have. Or a lot more. One or the other.

"So do you know the secret location where Sean Rivers is recovering from the rigours of being a child star, burned out at only fifteen?" Carl asked me, his tone suddenly intense.

"Yes, I mean no, no," I stuttered, looking anxiously at Jeremy. "I... haven't seen him in ages. I have no idea at all where he is living."

"Ruby and Sean were good friends on set, Carl," Jeremy stepped in smoothly. "But they haven't seen each other since filming wrapped. As far as we understand it, Sean is living peacefully in England enjoying life out of the spotlight. I'm sure that is exactly what all his fans want for him, so hopefully it will stay that way."

The audience applauded again and I closed my eyes for a second, feeling the heat in my face. I had broken my promise not to talk about Sean to anyone by talking about Sean to, well, most of America. Back home, everybody knew he went to Sylvia Lighthouse's Academy, but no one talked about it outside school because the academy has a very strict privacy and confidentially policy to protect its more famous students. (We've got a couple of princesses, a prime minister's son and one ex film star.) Everyone treated Sean like a normal boy and that was the way he liked it. Yes, I had broken my promise in front of twenty million people, but it was only because people were telling lies about him. I was sure he'd understand that. And I was fairly sure I didn't give away anything too important.

"You also worked with Imogene Grant on that film, didn't you, Ruby?" Carl asked me.

"Yes," I said, glad to be talking about anything else apart from Sean. "Imogene is a wonderful actress and an amazing person."

"Of course." Carl leant in close to me, cutting across Jeremy who was forced to lean backwards into the sofa. "Know any good secrets about Imogene?" he asked, waggling his brows. "Any reason why she's got a spring in her step and a sparkle in her eye recently? Any truth to those rumours that she has a new love in her life?"

"I do know a secret actually," I said, making the audience laugh again.

Jeremy looked at me. "Ruby, perhaps—" he began.

"You do? Is it a big secret?" Carl asked me gleefully, ignoring Jeremy.

"It's *massive*," I told him seriously with a slow nod of my head.

"Will it make the headlines in the morning?" Carl said, rubbing his hands together eagerly.

"It will," I said. "Although Imogene might kill me for telling you!"

"Come on, Ruby, spill it right here, right now!" Carl demanded, grinning at the studio audience. "What is this huge secret that Imogene has been hiding all of these months?"

"She likes full-fat mayonnaise on her cheese salad sandwich," I said.

The audience erupted into applause and laughter, and Carl reached out and shook my hand vigorously. Then I saw a man behind the camera making a "wind it up" motion with his hands and Carl turned to the autocue once more.

"Well that's all we've got time for tonight. Very many thanks to our guests, Christian Dane! Pete Peterson! Jeremy Fort! And tonight, ladies and gentleman, a star was born – Miss *Ruby* Parker!"

Hello Ruby,

How are you? Hope you had a good Christmas. We did. My brothers nearly killed each other again fighting over each other's presents, Dad ate so much he nearly exploded and Mum is moaning about the needles dropping off the Christmas tree!

Hi Ruby, this is me, Annie-Marie. My Christmas was OK in the end. Mum and Dad were actually back in the country at the same time so all four of us were sitting around the table for Christmas lunch, except that Mum didn't eat anything and Dad drank too much wine and Chris ate like a pig so he could leave early and go and see his girlfriend. Nobody really spoke to each other except to read the jokes out of the crackers which were rubbish so I sneaked away and spent the afternoon with Pilar, not that anyone seemed to notice. But I don't care because everything else is great. Sean is great. He sends his love and says he hopes they are not eating you alive in La-La Land (I think he means Los Angeles). I have some modelling work for H&M! By this summer you'll see me modelling their teen range in all the shops and magazines. Ah well, some of us have got it and some of us haven't...

OK, OK, enough from Annie. I have some news to tell you too. I've got a part in a new series for CBBC called *Totally Busted*. It's a sort of a cross between a comedy sketch show and a hidden camera show where we prank other kids. It's going to be really funny and it's very exciting. Jade and Menakshi are SICK with jealousy!

Anyway we want to know how many celebrities you have met? Looking forward to seeing you at home again soon for hot chocolate and girly gossip.

Nyds
and
Anne-Marie

PS Isn't it weird that Danny had a Christmas number one? He even beat the girl from *X Factor!* We can only pray that it will never happen again. (joking)

Chapter Six

I read Nydia and Anne-Marie's e-mail and was about to click on 'Reply' to tell them my incredible news when something made me stop and think.

After *The Carl Vine Show* I had been offered a really incredible opportunity, the kind that hardly ever happens to an average girl, even one who's been in a famous British soap and had a film role. But I'd barely had time to think about what it would mean to me or my life yet. I didn't want to tell anybody else until I had thought it through properly, no matter what everyone else wanted.

I could still hardly believe what had happened. Mum, Jeremy and I had all come out of the studio with Julian and the others and were waiting for the car to pick us up and take us back to Jeremy's. We were all on a high. The interview had gone really well, except for the bit where I nearly blew Sean's cover and I had hoped that everybody would forget about that. Mum seemed happy and relaxed again and really pleased with me, and Jeremy spoke on the phone to some people at Wide Open Universe and told me they were very pleased with me too.

Outside the celebrity entrance there were a few people waiting for autographs and Jeremy was signing, along with the man who had cried and Pete Peterson. I stood about for a bit, but nobody asked me for mine, which was fair enough because nobody knew who I was.

"Hey, I like you," Pete said, when he'd finished with his fans, pointing his finger and clicking his tongue at me. "You're a funny kid."

"Thanks," I said. "And you're a funny man."

"Oh, you kill me," Pete Peterson said, and then he climbed on to the back of a waiting motorbike and was gone.

Then, as Mum and I waited for Jeremy to finish, David started barking at something. It was a photographer taking photos with a long-distance lens.

"Paparazzi," Mum said in a low voice, almost a growl. "I'm not ready to be in any more magazines just yet."

"He'll be after Dane," Julian told her. "He's the hot ticket in town at the moment after his shocking fall from grace and his amazing ability to cry like a baby on national TV. Careers start and finish quickly in this town, but I think that was a record even for LA."

"Well, I think I'd rather wait inside until Jeremy is ready to leave, if you don't mind," Mum said, and so she, David and I went back into an area that was called "Stars' Reception". The walls of the room were lined with signed photos of celebrities who had been guests on the show. Considering that the show hadn't been on air that long there were already a lot of photos.

"Oh look, there's Imogene!" I said, going to her picture. They might retouch and paint out the so-called faults of other stars, but not Imogene. I knew her face well and the photograph reflected it exactly, including the faint crinkles around her eyes when she smiled and the mole on her chin.

Suddenly David started growling in my arms and I realised that there was someone standing behind me.

"Now, she's an old-style film star," a voice said in my ear. I turned and looked around at a quite old man in a dark pinstriped suit with not very much grey hair and a rather large pair of black-rimmed spectacles.

"It's Ruby, isn't it?" he asked me. I nodded and shook hands with him. His skin felt dry and papery, but he had a very strong grip.

"I'm Martin Blenheim of Blenheim Productions." He turned and shook my mother's hand too. "You might have heard of me?" I thought for a moment it sounded familiar, but I couldn't place it. I looked at Mum but her face was blank too.

"I'm sorry," I said. "Are you very famous?"

Mr Blenheim laughed, but it sounded more like a dry tickly cough.

"You could say that. The next time you're watching your favourite teen show, keep watching to the very end and you'll more than likely see that it's been produced by Blenheim Productions. My latest hit is *Hollywood High*."

"Oh, yes!" I said. "We haven't got it at home yet, but I read about some of the actresses in a magazine. It looks great!"

"We're lucky to have a very talented young cast. They all attend the Beaumont School of Performing Arts. We're halfway through shooting season two now, or at least we will be when the new semester starts."

"That sounds very interesting," I said politely.

"Good, I'm glad you're interested in me, Ruby, because I'm interested in you. I haven't spoken to your agent yet, but as you and your mother are right here I thought I might as well strike while the iron's hot, as you Brits say."

"Do we?" I asked, perplexed.

"We have a guest role on *Hollywood High* that urgently needs to be cast. It's the part of a girl called Isabella. She was originally supposed to be an Italian aristocrat, the daughter of a film director. She comes into the school and upsets the regular characters. People's boyfriends get interested in her and she turns friend against friend – the usual stuff. But she's a great character – a real villain, the kind you love to hate. Unfortunately, the girl we cast has had to pull out at the last minute because of family problems. We are on the verge of rewriting all of those episodes; in fact, we may have already started. But then I watched you tonight and I had an idea. We could transform Isabella into Lady Elizabeth, an uppercrust English girl. And I thought you'd be perfect for the part."

"Who me?" I said, looking first at my mum and then back at Mr Blenheim. "Oh no, I'm sorry, Mr Blenheim. I can't take the part – I'm only here on holiday!"

"Of course we'd need to see a showreel and screen-test you with the other actors," Mr Blenheim went on regardless. "But given we could sort out the visa and schooling issues, and get the whole production team on board, then I'm certain that you are a fit for the part. I have an instinct about you and my instinct is never wrong."

"I'm sorry, Mr Blenheim," my mum stepped in at last, "but Ruby is right. We're only here for another few days and then we're flying back to London. Your offer is an amazing one, but I need to think about Ruby's schoolwork. This year is an important one for her."

"Mrs Parker," Mr Blenheim smiled so that his whole face seemed to turn into a mass of creases, "please don't dismiss this chance for your daughter out of hand. Yes, you need to give my proposal serious thought, but I really think that the issues you are worried about are things we could resolve. You'd only need to extend your stay here by around six weeks, perhaps a little longer. The character I want Ruby for features in six episodes and it takes a week to shoot an episode on a tight schedule. There are laws, you know, about how long the young cast can work. The school day at Beaumont starts at 8 a.m. and finishes at 1 p.m. We shoot on location at the school and at the nearby studios in the afternoon."

"Mr Blenheim, you have to give Ruby and I a moment to adjust. The offer you've made is quite a shock. I can see how great it would be for Ruby's career, but Ruby has to keep up with her studies," my mum said. "She'll be starting work on her GCSE coursework this year."

"Well," Mr Blenheim rubbed his chin thoughtfully. "It would be possible to enrol Ruby temporarily at the Beaumont School." Both he and my mother seemed completely oblivious to me. "And we could get her curriculum sent over so that she wouldn't fall behind.

She could slot right back into her studies when she gets home. What do you think, Ruby?" He turned to me at last and smiled, clearly not put off by the dumbstruck expression I must have had on my face. Maybe he couldn't tell underneath all that make-up.

"I... um... well..." I honestly didn't know what to think, but as it turned out I didn't have to; my mum was doing all the thinking for me.

"Mr Blenheim, you've convinced me – like you said, this is far too good a chance for her to pass up. Ruby would be happy to audition for the part of Lady Elizabeth and we'll worry about her GCSEs when we have to – and who needs GCSEs to be a film and TV star anyway?"

I stared at my mum and could not stop my jaw from dropping. Something really radical was changing in her and it wasn't just her giant pout. Perhaps it was the shock and hurt of seeing her photograph portrayed so unkindly in the magazine. Maybe it was the pressure of trying to be Jeremy Fort's girlfriend when you knew his ex was a supermodel. Or it might have been something more, something in the air or the water in this town, a kind of nameless hunger to succeed. But one thing I knew for certain, before we came on our holiday to Hollywood, it would have been me begging her to let me audition for the part in *Hollywood High*, and her putting her foot down, telling me that school was still more important than anything else. And never, *never* in a millions years would the old mum have allowed a sentence that included the words "who needs GSCEs" to cross her lips.

I had to face it. My normal, sensible-shoe-wearing and quite often annoying mother had morphed into a wrinkleless, big-haired Hollywood mom overnight.

I looked at her with her new glamorous blonde locks and tight orange skin and wondered how I could tell her that, as crazy as it might seem, I wasn't sure if I *wanted* to audition for the show. Suddenly, the prospect of one of my many acting-related dreams coming true seemed too frightening and too quick. I wasn't ready. I was on holiday for goodness sake! We'd only been here a little while and look what had happened already. My mum had gone all Stepford Wives and I hadn't exactly been the nicest person to be around.

Plus it would mean another six weeks away from home. Another six weeks without seeing or having a chance to make up with Dad. Without Everest or Nydia or Annie-Marie. And another six weeks without seeing Danny, a thought that made me feel as if there was a huge, heavy, cold pebble in the pit of my stomach.

Apart from anything else, I was actually looking forward to going back to school. Returning to my nice, safe, normal life, or as normal as things ever get for a child actress who goes to stage school. I missed sitting at the back of lessons thinking that my head might implode from boredom, or hanging out with Danny and the girls at break time, watching Anne-Marie and Jade's latest sparring session that Anne-Marie always won. And although I'd only been gone a couple of weeks, I was even getting all nostalgic about the thought of walking home in the wet and the cold to watch *Deal Or No Deal*, doing my homework and going to bed.

OK, maybe my life might not be most people's idea of normal. After all, my first film was soon to be released in the UK and my boyfriend was now a pop star as well as a soap star. (Not forgetting that one of my best friends was going out with possibly the most famous boy on the planet while he was living out of the public eye.) But it was mine. And I liked it.

I smiled at Mr Blenheim. "The thing is… I mean, I'm sure it would be great," I said. "It's just a… surprise. I need to think about it very carefully and talk to Ms Lighthouse and—"

"When do you want Ruby to audition?" my mum said, talking right over the top of me so that it didn't seem worth finishing my sentence. I got the feeling that my opinion wasn't that important any more.

While Mum and Mr Blenheim talked I peered outside to the parking lot and saw that the crowds and the photographers had gone. There was only Jeremy's silver Rolls Royce waiting for us with Jeremy sitting patiently in it chatting to Lisa Wells.

"Ah, Ruby," he said as I climbed into the car, "what's going on?"

"Mum's talking to a TV producer," I said, not wanting to elaborate just then.

"Networking, eh?" Jeremy said with a fond smile. "Sometimes I think I should employ your mother as my manager. Julian and his colleagues have gone back to pick up all the clothes and things they left at the house. They said you can keep what you're wearing. The clothing company had a representative at the taping and they say that you were exactly the kind of girl they wanted to see in their clothes. I think Julian said they might be sending you some more free items too."

"Really? That's great!" I said, having to force enthusiasm. Normally, the thought of free stuff would make me want to cartwheel with joy. Free stuff was the only thing better in the world than shopping for stuff. But as I looked at the doorway where Mum was still talking I wondered what she and Mr Blenheim had in store for me and, more importantly, why I wasn't excited about it.

"Ruby," Lisa said, leaning over Jeremy to kiss me on both cheeks, "I just wanted to tell you that Art and Mr Honeycutt and the whole studio are thrilled with your performance tonight. They are already talking about getting you on more talkshows in the few days you have left here – so don't you worry, we are going to *make* this film a hit."

"Thanks, Lisa," I said as she climbed out of the car. Actually, I hadn't been that worried about the success of the film until I saw the look in Lisa's eyes when she reassured me and I realised how worried *she* was. I was too busy worrying about my amazing opportunity to guest star in *Hollywood High*.

"That went pretty well, didn't it?" Jeremy said, picking up his paper. "Now we just have to hope your mother will wrap up her wheeler-dealing in time for supper. Augusto is making risotto, just for you."

"Jeremy?" I asked him after a moment. He raised a brow in reply. "Do you think Mum is OK?"

He laughed and his paper rattled. "I think she's fine, Ruby. She's taken to Hollywood like a duck to water."

That's what I was afraid of.

I picked up the magazine I'd bought that morning, a time that seemed like a million years away, and opened it at the photos of Adrienne Charles and Nadine Navarro.

Adrienne was a beautiful shiny blonde with blue eyes that seemed to sparkle on the page. Nadine's skin looked like polished ebony and her long hair hung in shining curls. Both girls had smiles that could blind you if you stared at them directly. Neither one would want to be friends with me in a million years. Not me with my only normally white teeth and my hair that was mostly a mess and skin that broke out every three weeks or so. It was true that I had once thought the same about Anne-Marie and now she and I were best friends, but as pretty as Anne-Marie is, even she is not as glossy or as polished as these girls. Anne-Marie was real. Adrienne and Nadine were *unreal*.

I have seen probably every single high-school movie that has ever been made in the last five years and I know exactly what happens to girls like me at high school. They get eaten alive. Unpopular, geeky, nerdy, a loser. All of those words had been used to describe me at one time or another. And I was certain that this time would be no different.

Of course I could be wrong. I am good at being wrong about things and people; it's one of my best things. Maybe Nadine would be sweet and shy and Adrienne would be a secret *Kensington Heights* fan. Perhaps it *could* be exciting and an amazing new step in my acting career.

And it wasn't forever. Just another six weeks out here instead of being at home, with hot chocolate, Everest and the mess I keep hiding underneath my bed instead of putting it away like Mum keeps asking me to. At least in Hollywood somebody else tidies up my room.

Mum finally got in the car and started telling Jeremy everything. I realised then that I was the only one who wasn't sure about this, which had to mean that my worries were all silly and pointless. Didn't it?

I closed Nydia's e-mail and looked at myself in the full-length mirror in my bedroom. The pristine clothes I had worn for a few hours were already grubby, my hair had frizzed up and the thick layer of so-called natural-look foundation that Julian had caked on my face had actually cracked in a few places.

And then I realised, Mr Blenheim had seen the fully made up and primped up version of me on *The Carl Vine Show*. I had been putting on an accent that wasn't mine and looking like I can *never* look unless I have three personal stylists following me around all of the time refreshing my lip gloss and pulling me out of the way of potential stainage situations. It would be all right, I realised suddenly, to go and audition because when Mr Blenheim saw me with no make-up on and in my own "cheap tat" clothes, he would realise that I was about as far away from being an English lady as was possible. And if I did the audition and failed, at least Mum would be happy that I'd tried. It was always Mum that said that trying and doing my best was the main thing, and that it wouldn't be the end of the world if I didn't get a part. Then I could go home and forget all about *Hollywood High* until I watched it on TV on a Sunday morning over my cereal.

I washed off as much of the make-up on my face as I could in one go and went downstairs to find Mum. She was on the phone in Jeremy's study so I waited by the sofa for her to finish her call.

"That's great, marvellous – I'm so pleased, speak soon. Bye!" She put the receiver down and held out her arms. I ran to her and hugged her tight, glad to know that she was still my soft, round mum under that orange skin.

"I've been thinking," I said, smiling at her. "I will give that audition a go for *Hollywood High*. I mean I can only try my best, right?"

My mum laughed, her eyes sparkling with excitement. "Of course you are doing the audition, darling. I've already made all of the arrangements so you don't have to worry about anything except being brilliant and I know you won't let me down on that score. I've spoken to Audrey and to Ms Lighthouse and both of them say they can certainly work with Blenheim Productions if you get through the auditions, which I know you will."

I tried to interrupt, but she was in full flow. I don't think I had ever seen her this excited about anything, not even when I auditioned for *The Lost Treasure of King Arthur*. My mum was usually so determined that I keep my feet on the ground and have a normal life. Not this time.

"Now I was thinking," Mum went on, releasing me from my hug to pace the floor of Jeremy's office. "When Mr Blenheim saw you on the show you had had your hair and make-up done and those nice clothes, which is not really like you at all so—"

"So he might not want me when he sees the real me and we might have to forget about it," I said, trying and failing not to sound hopeful.

"No, darling." Mum ruffled my hair in exactly the way she knew I didn't like, only this time I think she'd forgotten that I didn't like it and wasn't just doing it for a joke like she normally does. "Illusion – that's what acting is all about. I phoned Lisa and got Julian's number and called him. He says he can definitely get you more clothes from that label, and that he'll come and do your hair and make-up again, and come with us to the audition to keep you looking good. So all you have to do is to turn up and be brilliant." She turned to me. "Ruby, I will be so proud of you."

I looked at my mum, her face full of excitement and her eyes glittering. She had thought of everything to try and get me this part and I couldn't work out why it was that I was feeling so down about it. OK, I was scared and nervous of going to a new school and walking on to a new set. But it would only be for a while, and no matter what my tummy thought about it, my head told me that this was an amazing opportunity. It was one that I had to stop being uncertain about and give a hundred per cent to, even if only for my mum, because she would be so proud of me if I did this.

"It's going to be fantastic, Mum," I said, bouncing a little on my toes. "It's going to be fantastic – it really, really is!"

And I kept on saying it until I started to believe it too.

HOLLYWOOD HIGH©

A BLENHEIM PRODUCTIONS PRODUCTION

SEASON TWO EPISODE 23

"THE PRINCESS AND THE FOOTBALL PLAYER"

WRITTEN BY: SUZIE BLENHEIM, JENNY
ROBERTS, SAM JENKINS, HALLE GONZALEZ,
NAVEEN SMITH AND CONNIE KREMER

DIRECTED BY: SUZIE BLENHEIM

SCENE 48

INT. LUNCH RECESS, THE CAFETERIA

NATALIE and SABRINA are sitting with
PARMINDER and LARA at their usual table.
They are in close discussion when Sabrina
looks up to middle distance and notices
that the subject of their discussion is
approaching their table.

> **SABRINA**
> Shhh, girls - she's coming
> over!

The table is quiet as all four girls look up. Their faces are less than friendly.

LADY ELIZABETH

Hello? Would you mind awfully if I came over and sat down with you ladies? I expect you know it's my first day at school here in America and as I'm sure you can imagine it is rather different from my old girls' school.

SABRINA

(Coldly)Is it true that you really are a "Lady" and that we all have to call you "Lady" Elizabeth?

LADY ELIZABETH

(Sits down despite lack of invitation) Goodness no! I mean, yes, formally I do

have the title of "Lady"
but nobody, not even our
servants, calls me Lady
anything. Please just call
me Lizzy. I might have a
different accent and come
from a faraway land but
really I am just like you.
Right now I could really
use some friends and it's
easy to see that you
ladies are the coolest
girls in your grade. I'd
be so grateful if you
would agree to show me the
ropes as it were?

NATALIE
Do you know the princes?

LADY ELIZABETH
Of course I know the
princes. My older brother
Edgar goes to Sandhurst with
them.

The girls look at each other and make an almost telepathic decision.

                    NATALIE
          OK, you're in.

                  LADY ELIZABETH
          Oh, this is going to be
          jolly good fun!

But there is a glint in LADY ELIZABETH'S eyes that tells us she's going to be trouble.

Chapter Seven

I suppose that I expected my only second ever professional audition to be something like the first. When I auditioned for *The Lost Treasure of King Arthur* it hadn't been glamorous at all, at least not the first time. We all had to wait in a grubby corridor above a shop in Soho and then troop one by one into a whitewashed dance studio where a panel of people who I thought were utterly terrifying (so terrifying that I actually threw up) were waiting for me.

So when the day of the audition arrived, I was prepared for it to be more or less the same. Not in a dance studio above a shop, but gut-wrenchingly terrifying. And in a funny kind of way, the terrifying part was the only thing that was certain about the whole experience. Because I *certainly* didn't know how to feel about it.

We had only been in Hollywood a little while, and though it was wonderful and exciting in so many ways, it had been eventful enough for me already. And now there was a steely glint in Mum's eye and a kind of determination to change everything, including my life, that I had seen somewhere before but couldn't quite put my finger on.

But despite her oddness, it was a new experience to have Mum so totally behind me going for a part. Especially one that would mean more time away from school and home and the life where my feet were anchored firmly to the ground in exactly the place where Mum most liked them to be. For once I wasn't getting the "It's not the end of the world if you don't get it" speech or her "There'll be other parts, Ruby, and you're still so young – you have all the time in the world" talk. And funnily enough, for the first time ever, I wanted to hear both of them.

More than that I wanted her to ask me the question she always asked me and to which up until now I had always replied "Yes". I wanted her to ask me if I was sure if this was what I really wanted.

But she didn't.

I decided to phone Dad that evening after Mum told me that the audition was all arranged. I hadn't spoken to him since we left and I didn't think that my rather rude conversation with his so-called girlfriend had done anything to help how we had left things between us. I wanted to hear his voice. I wanted to say sorry and for him to be OK with me again and call me "kiddo" and tell me a terrible joke.

Part of me wanted to tell him that I was unsure about auditioning for *Hollywood High* but I felt that if I did, if I said anything about how Mum had changed then I would be being disloyal to her. Still I wanted to tell Dad about the audition, no matter how I felt about it, just so that I could hear in his voice whether or not he thought it was a good idea. But when I picked up the phone and dialled, all I heard on the other end was the ringing tone. I wondered if I was getting Dad out of bed because I wasn't really sure what the time was back home, but I was pretty certain that he would be there.

He didn't pick up though and I wondered if it was because he knew it was me and didn't want to speak to me. Or if it was because he had stayed the night at his so-called girlfriend's place. I felt a rush of anger and slammed the receiver down hard. If that was true, if he was at her place, then he wasn't at home wishing he could make friends with me. He wasn't even thinking about me. He was taking another step further away and I wondered how long it would be before he was gone from my life forever.

I didn't try and call Danny or e-mail the others. I didn't want to say anything to them until I knew if I would be offered the part. It was partly superstition, wanting to keep it to myself as if even talking about the audition might jinx it. Also, despite my misgivings, the competitive part of me still wanted to do well. Chances like this were, after all, what I had devoted my short career to so far.

The main reason I didn't tell them anything though was because I didn't want my life to change any more than it already had. My friends were waiting for me to come home in a few days and somehow this fact made that life still real. If I rang them and told them that actually I might not be home for weeks or even months, then they would stop waiting for me, stop expecting me. There would stop being a gap at the lunch table or space at my desk in class because the everyday life I was no longer part of would gradually close over and cover my absence.

Chapter Eight

A few hours before we had to leave for Blenheim Studios, Julian arrived with my audition "costume". He claimed he had done a lot of research before he finally unveiled the outfit he was confident would nail me the part.

I dutifully took it to my room and put it on, wearing it back down to the living room where Mum, Julian and Jeremy were waiting. Jeremy smiled.

"I would say that is *exactly* the Hollywood perception of a young English Lady," he said, winking at me. I was wearing a pale blue cotton shirt with the collar turned up so that it flapped just beneath my ears, and a string of pearls over that. Julian had insisted that I tuck the shirt into the blue and green tartan skirt that came to just about my knees, pulling half of it out so that it billowed over the waistband. Then he made me put on a pair of pristine white *knee socks*, the sort I hadn't worn since primary school, and finally he strapped on a pair of black patent leather round-toed shoes with a t-bar.

"Perfect," he said.

"Do you get *Hiya! Bye-a!* over here?" I asked him cautiously.

Julian looked puzzled. "We get the American version," he said.

"Oh, well, it's just that in the British version you quite often see photos of real Lady This or That and stories about actual Right Honourable Miss Blahs, and they never, EVER look like... like... this."

"Yes," Julian said smartly. "But this isn't about how your English aristocrats really look; it's about how we Americans expect them to look. And *this* is how."

Of course Blenheim Studios was nothing like the dance place where I auditioned for *The Lost Treasure of King Arthur*. Much more modern than Wide Open Universe, it consisted of several new and shiny-looking buildings covered in reflective glass windows, but its avenues were still lined with the palm trees that I had now got used to seeing everywhere.

A woman in a cream trouser suit was waiting for us when we arrived and introduced herself as Karen Miller. "Follow me, please," she said, leading us across an open forecourt into a separate building. "Mr Blenheim and Suzie thought it would be nice to audition you on set with the other actors in costume and make-up, to help you really get a feel for what it would be like to be part of *Hollywood High*."

I swallowed, but my mouth was so dry there was nothing to go down, so my tongue stuck to the roof of my mouth. I wished more than anything that I could turn around and run away in the opposite direction, back to where Jeremy's air-conditioned car was waiting along with David, who was no doubt angrily making a hole in the upholstery. I would ask Jeremy to take me straight to the airport so that I could home and find my fat and friendly cat, Everest, and get into bed and pull the covers over our heads and hide. But I knew that I couldn't. I knew that I had to go through with this and there was nothing that could stop it.

It was the cafeteria set that Karen led us to. Unlike the sets on *Kensington Heights* which looked pretty small and really fake in real life, it was a huge set kitted out as far as I could see in perfect detail down to the lunch counter. There was enough room for at least fifty extras and for camera crews to move around, which made the filming seem more natural and less static. And it was lit as if bright Hollywood sunshine was streaming in through the windows, even though there were none. I couldn't help but be impressed; I had never been on a set like this before. And for the first time, the thought of working somewhere like this set a buzzing feeling of excitement vibrating in my chest.

We saw Mr Blenheim talking to some crew and Karen led us over to him. I looked but I couldn't see any of the other actors yet.

"Ruby!" Mr Blenheim's mouth stretched into a wide papery grin as he held out his hand for me to shake. His dry grip was firm as he gestured at the dark-haired woman standing next to him. "Thank you so much for coming in. This is Suzie, my daughter and the series director. Suzie originated *Hollywood High* and still helps write a lot of the episodes. Since you and I last talked, Audrey Gold sent us your showreel and we are both very impressed."

"We sure are," Suzie Blenheim said, taking my hand in both of hers and smiling. "Gary, will you get the girls on set, please," Suzie asked a tall and stringy young man who seemed to be her assistant. She beamed at me. "Let's get started!"

Moments later I met Adrienne and Nadine. Well I say "met": it was more that they launched themselves at me and hugged me, both of them squealing like overexcited mice, as if they'd known me all their lives. It was overwhelming and unexpected but also very nice, because all at once I didn't feel quite so terrified any more. Still *fairly* petrified, but not like I might drop dead at any second.

"Wow, Ruby, it's *so* great to meet you," Adrienne said, swinging my hand in hers.

"Word is that you are the next big thing," Nadine told me, with a huge sparkly-toothed smile.

"Um, well... I'm not sure about that," I mumbled.

"Is it true that you and Imogene Grant are really good friends?" Adrienne asked. "I'd so love to meet Imogene Grant one day. Can you introduce us?"

"Well, maybe," I said. "But I think she's going to Hungary to shoot her next film soon..."

"And your mom is dating Jeremy Fort, right?" Nadine added. "I wish my mom would date someone classy and British. I'm so bored of male American TV stars; they basically all look the same anyway." Both girls laughed and so did I, not because I thought all male American TV stars look the same, but because if Nadine and Adrienne were laughing then I wanted to laugh. I wanted to do whatever they were doing.

I was utterly amazed by how normal and friendly they were, although I realised, I shouldn't be. After all, what they did every day wasn't that different from what I used to do on *Kensington Heights* and I am *mostly* quite normal and friendly. Also, for a long time I judged Anne-Marie on how she looked. I thought anybody that beautiful couldn't be a nice person too (and to be fair, the fact that she despised me didn't help improve our relationship). But then I got to know her and she got to know me, and we realised that actually we were OK. By which I mean that despite first impressions we could be friends after all. So maybe it would be possible for me to be friends with these two bouncy, shiny, golden beings.

"OK, girls," Suzie said quite firmly. "Enough of the gossip; there'll be plenty of time to get to that later. Let's run through the scene. Take your places! Camera rolling and... action!"

After the scene had wrapped and the grown-ups were standing round a monitor reviewing the tape, Adrienne, Nadine and I stayed sitting at the canteen table.

"Ruby," Nadine said with half a smile, lowering her voice, "what *did* your mom make you wear today! No offence, but you look like a reject from the last century."

I laughed; she was right after all. "It wasn't Mum, it was my stylist. Well, he's not exactly *my* stylist. Mum thought that because Mr Blenheim saw me all dressed up and doing a posh voice on *The Carl Vine Show* that I should do it again only more so…"

"I *love* your accent, it's so cool," Nadine said. "You'll have to teach me how to do a really good British accent while you're here, OK?"

"*If* I'm here," I said ruefully.

"You'll be here. Anyway, your stylist was wrong. We get British *Vogue* and *Tatler* over here too, you know. Your English aristocracy is very classy. We especially like your princes." She smiled at me mischievously. "I don't suppose you know them too?"

I shook my head and smiled. "No, sorry," I said. "I went to Buckingham Palace on a field trip once though."

The girls laughed. I'd clearly said something really witty. I just wasn't sure what.

"You'll love school; it's so cool, not like any other school you've ever been too," Nadine told me. "And there are some seriously cute guys too, especially the ones who work with us on the show."

"Oh, I'm going out with someone," I said with a shrug.

"Going out where?" Adrienne asked, looking faintly puzzled.

"I mean I already have a boyfriend at home," I said, feeling suddenly shy. "Danny Harvey." Nadine and Adrienne looked blankly at me and I supposed that they had never heard of Danny. Well that was OK because I was fairly sure that he had never heard of them either. "He's just had a number one hit back in Britain," I said, feeling the need to boast on Danny's behalf.

"Really? So you date a pop star. Cool," Adrienne said. "Of course we've got four of them in our school. They're in a band. Envision. They've been signed but they're not really huge – not yet."

I shook my head. "I haven't heard of them."

"Well that's OK," Adrienne said. "You will. They're going to play at our Valentine's dance – hey, you'll be here for the Valentine's dance. We'll have to get you a date."

"Well, I…" The girls were going too fast for me.

"You can't go without a date," Nadine told me. "Well, you can, but it's seriously not cool. Look, don't worry, stick with us and you'll be very popular at Beaumont. Finding you a date will be easy."

"Or it will be once you've escaped from that outfit," Adrienne giggled. And as the three of us laughed, again I suddenly felt excited about the prospect of going to a real American high school (even if it was a theatre school) and working on a real American TV show and even maybe going to a real American Valentine's dance. I had no sense of how I'd done in the audition, but caught up in the moment and in Nadine and Adrienne's friendliness, I really, *really* wanted to be offered the part of Lady Elizabeth.

"Ruby," Suzie Blenheim smiled at me as she came over. I searched the smile for any hint of what it might mean. Was it a "Sorry you didn't make it" smile or a "Yes, you're hired" one? It seemed to hover somewhere in between the two.

My mum hurried over to join us.

"Thank you so much for coming in today. You've done really good work." Suzie paused and looked from me to my mother. "I'm afraid I can't tell you yet if you have the part. I know I want you for it and Dad *loves* you, but it's going to take a while before we can let you know for sure."

"Suzie!" Adrienne exclaimed. "Can't you say now? Please? *I* want her to get the part!"

Suzie smiled that level smile again. "Adrienne, you know I can't. Now, you girls, the rest of the cast is in make-up right now so go and make sure you're ready for your next scene, OK?"

"Yes, ma'am," Adrienne said, giving me a quick hug before she ran off.

"What do you Brits say? Oh, yeah, 'break an arm', Ruby!" Nadine called over her shoulder, blowing me a kiss as she followed Adrienne.

"So is that all for now?" my mum said, and I knew she would have been frowning if she could have made her brows go together.

"That's all for now," Suzie said. "Karen will take you to your car and we'll be in touch as soon as possible."

"I hope you are," my mum said quite sharply. "Because my daughter is very much in demand, Ms Blenheim, so if you want her, you'd better make sure you get her soon."

"Mum!" I exclaimed before I could stop myself, shocked at her blatant lie – the only thing that was going to be demanded of me when I got home was some homework and getting picked second from last for netball.

"We'll speak very soon, Mrs Parker," Suzie said, holding out her hand to end the conversation.

Mum and I followed Karen back to the car where, as soon as he saw us, David began flinging himself against the gap in the window, sticking his snarling and barking little muzzle through it. I was beginning to see that this was his way of telling us that he was pleased to see us.

Once we were in the car I rounded on Mum. "Why did you say that to Suzie – that I was in demand?" I asked as David climbed up my shoulder and nipped at my ear. "You know I'm not."

"Because you have to play hardball to get results," my mum said. Yes, my mum, Janice Parker, actually did say that.

I did a double-take and peered closely at her.

"Mum," I asked her cautiously. "Why are you suddenly so desperate for me to get this role? You've always been pretty relaxed about my career before. Always told me that I don't need to go so fast, that I'm only a child and all of that business."

Mum looked at me again, with the steely glint in her eye that had worried me so much before, and said, "We might have only been here a couple of weeks, Ruby, but that's all it's taken for me to realise something. This business you want to be part of, that you've *worked* to be part of since you were a little girl, isn't nice. It isn't fluffy and cuddly. It's hard and it's difficult and sometimes it's cruel. And if you want to find true success, then it's here, in this town, where you will find it and have the level of recognition that you deserve. This part is a guest role, but if audiences like you, it could become more – maybe even your own series."

"I seriously doubt it," I said. "And anyway, even if I did, we'd have to live here, like, properly."

"Obviously," Mum said, rolling her eyes.

And as I looked at her I realised where I'd seen that look before. It had been on Pat Rivers' face. Sean's dad, the man who worked him so cruelly and hard that he began to hate acting and gave up his enormous fame, possibly forever, running away to hide from the world. That was how my mum looked just then. And it frightened me.

"What if I don't want this role," I said quietly.

"Don't be silly, Rubes," my mum said, looking out of the window. "Of course you want it. And you'll get it. Wait and see."

Hip Hip Hooray for the Hunks!

As the New Year rolls in we list the Top Ten reasons why you should feel happy to be alive. They're hot, they're young and they're all still technically available. So make sure you keep on the lookout, girls. These are the guys worth catching!

1 He won a nation of teenage hearts with his mean and moody portrayal of *Kensington Heights* Bad Boy, Marcus Ridley, and now he's serenaded us with his dreamy chart-topping release *Kensington Heights (You take me to…)*. Yes it's true, he's been linked with former *Kensington Heights* star Ruby Parker who, rumour has it, is trying to make it in Hollywood. But if she's not in the country, we don't think she counts as a girlfriend. What greater achievement could there be for Danny Harvey? He's topped our chart of handsome hunks to hip-hip hooray for, that's what!

2 For a while there we went off another *Kensington Heights* hotty, Justin de Souza. But since he's had that haircut and that great new storyline, we at *Teen Girl!* think he's almost back on top. Almost! Those blue eyes still wow us and that dazzling smile is second to none. For old times' sake Justin comes in at number two.

3 Who says *Hollyoaks* hasn't got what it takes to deliver truly talented totty any more.

Dear Rubes, hello babe!

I just tore this out of 'Teen Girl!' for you to see about Danny. It's so funny, isn't it? Girls are going mad for him. I suppose he told you that he had nearly 6000 Christmas cards and I heard applications to the Academy have gone through the roof, tons of girls trying to go to school with the love of their life. And it's only Danny, with his rubbish jokes and awful voice. If they knew Sean went to the Academy too – I hate to think what would happen!

Anyway you'd better come back soon before an army of little girls carry him away for good.

Love Annie xxx

PS I sort of like being called Annie now. It's down to Sean really. The TRUE chart-topping hunk around here!

Chapter Nine

There were only two days left until we were officially supposed to go home when Anne-Marie's note arrived, with the article from *Teen Girl!* ripped out and paperclipped to it.

I was glad to see her handwriting on the envelope, even if my boyfriend being at the top of a chart of Handsome Hunks didn't exactly cheer me up. Especially not when Mum was considering rebooking our return flights home, even though we had not yet heard either way about the audition yet.

I unfolded the magazine article and looked at the photo of Danny that was included in the piece. It was the one where he was resting his chin on crossed arms and staring moodily into the camera as if no one in the whole world could really understand him. He was very good at doing misunderstood; that's what girls loved about him, each of them certain that they could be the one to do all the understanding. Funny though, because the real Danny, once you got to know him, was about as different from the boy in this photo as he possibly could be. He wasn't moody, he was shy, and he wasn't arrogant or stuck up. He was friendly and probably the most normal teen pop sensation in the history of the world.

I almost pressed the photo to my lips until I realised that probably a few thousand girls had also done the same thing, dreaming about having Danny as a boyfriend. But I didn't have to dream. Somehow, he actually was my boyfriend. Only I was thousands of miles away and not sure if I would be going back home any time soon.

Nobody, not even my former mum and certainly not my present one, had to tell me that the age of thirteen wasn't a time to be throwing away amazing chances like guest-starring in a top-rating US TV show just because I missed my boyfriend. And I really wanted the part now. Not just because I thought that Mum might actually implode and disown me if I didn't get it (not necessarily in that order). But also because Adrienne and Nadine had both been so nice to me that I thought going to school with them for a few weeks would be exciting and fun.

But that didn't help the fact that I got jealous when Danny was listed in polls like the one in *Teen Girl!*, or when I found out (*not* from Danny) that he got six thousand Christmas cards. I'd felt that way before and Danny had told me then that it was crazy to be jealous of people he had never even met. But I was sure that it wouldn't be that long before he met someone who was a lot prettier, a lot funnier and a lot nearer to him than I was. He was only thirteen too, after all. He wasn't exactly going to be waiting for me all of his life.

Still, I would be seeing him soon, even if I didn't go home in two days. The night after the audition I had e-mailed Nydia, Anne-Marie, Sean and Danny and told them about everything that had happened, including the possibility that I might get a guest role in *Hollywood High*.

They had all e-mailed me back overnight. Nydia told me that it would be fantastic if I got it, but that she would miss me. Anne-Marie informed me that Nadine Navarro had featured in the Gap modelling campaign last year and wanted me to tell her what Nadine's skin looked like close up. Sean warned me not to let Hollywood suck me in and to remind myself that I was still just a kid. And finally, an e-mail from Danny which said he'd be keeping his fingers crossed for me. And then he asked me if I had a webcam because he'd just got one for his computer at his dad's house and if I had one, then we'd be able to see each other face to face.

I had run to ask Jeremy, who arranged for one to be delivered and fitted the same day, and I had to admit to myself that being the daughter of a film star's girlfriend was not all that bad.

This evening was to be our scheduled web chat. It would be my bedtime and Danny's breakfast time and I couldn't wait to see his face. (And ask him about those six thousand Christmas cards.)

Something to look forward to seemed very important because the atmosphere in Jeremy's house since I had done the audition was tense, stretched like a balloon on the verge of popping.

Mum's tan had faded quite a lot so that she no longer looked orange, just a sort of pale yellowy colour. The swelling had gone down on her mouth too, so that I could finally see glimpses of her old self under her glamorous new appearance. But instead of just waiting nervously with me, thinking up ways to distract me and reminding me how nice life was for a normal thirteen-year-old, she launched a military style operation that should have been entitled "Operation Get Ruby Famous". I overheard her talking to Audrey in London, listened as she made appointments with casting agents and bookers, and once I even caught her asking Jeremy what contacts he could use to get me another part if *Hollywood High* didn't work out. I could see that Jeremy was reluctant to get involved, but Mum didn't seem to notice. So in the end he said he'd see what he could do, but I think it was mainly so that Mum would stop asking.

"Mum," I'd said to her one morning as she pored over Jeremy's computer checking her e-mails, "I thought this *Hollywood High* was a one-off. A chance that came out of the blue. I didn't think... I mean, we aren't moving here for good, are we?"

Mum looked up. "Mr Blenheim offering you that audition just made me think that while we're here we should explore our options, Ruby," she said, as if the question irritated her. "I've been underestimating you and what you are capable of achieving. I suppose I got used to you working on *Kensington Heights*. I took it for granted and didn't see how special you were. And when you got the part in the film, I didn't really understand what it could mean for us, for you, I mean. But I'm here for you now and I've seen how this town works... and I think that you are just as good as any other girl out there, Ruby. In fact, I think you are better. And I want you to reach your full potential."

"Reach my full potential?" I repeated the alien-sounding phrase nervously.

And then I had finally said what I hadn't quite been able to before.

"Mum, if I don't get the part of Lady Elizabeth, I want to go home. I want to go back to The Academy. I don't want to live in Hollywood. I mean, what about home and Dad and my GCSEs and my friends? I'm just not ready."

Mum had smiled at me and held out her arms, and I went over and sat on her lap like a big baby and rested my head on her shoulder. As she hugged me I felt an enormous sense of relief, like my worries had floated right off the top of my head.

"Listen, darling," she said. "You don't have to worry about anything. I know what's best for you. And I think that staying in Hollywood is exactly that."

I was so surprised by what she said and so shocked by the weight of fear crashing back down on to my shoulders that I didn't say anything. Because if Mum hadn't understood what I had just said, then what was the point of saying anything more?

"Up you get then," Mum said, shoving me off her lap. "Some of us need to get on."

I tore the photo of Danny carefully out of the magazine article and tucked it into my jeans pocket, where David immediately tried to retrieve it in order to eat it, no doubt. Since Jeremy had taken us to all the tourist hotspots during our two weeks here, and we had shopped until we had literally dropped of exhaustion, we hadn't really done that much for the last day or so except hang around the house and wait for Blenheim studios to call.

I had discovered American TV and had been watching reruns of the first series of *Hollywood High*. The more I watched it, the more I wanted to be in it. It had me hooked from the beginning. The words that came out of each character's mouth were much cleverer and funnier than any I had ever heard a real teen say, but if I got a chance to say lines like that, I didn't care whether it was realistic or not.

My other favourite new telly find was C! the Celebrity Channel. It had story after story about who was going out with whom, who'd adopted whom from which country, and who was now not going out with whom, and more, on a rolling basis. I was sitting on the floor with David on my lap, flicking through the million or so channels that there seemed to be when I stopped on C! because I remembered there was going to be a documentary on the making of *Hollywood High* and I wanted to check what time it was on. It was in the middle of a story and a yellow banner ran along the bottom of the screen which read: STAR'S SECRET HIDEAWAY FOUND!

There was an aerial shot, probably taken from a helicopter, of a building that seemed familiar to me. I stared at it, getting a funny feeling of unease in the pit of my tummy. It was definitely a building somewhere in Britain, an old white stone building with turrets and towers – maybe some kind of castle that I had visited once on a school trip or something. And then, as the helicopter flew lower and I saw the front of the building at a different angle, I realised. It wasn't a building I had visited, it was a building that I knew like the back of my hand because I went there almost every single day.

It was Sylvia Lighthouse's Academy for the Performing Arts.

I turned up the volume, sat down heavily on the floor and listened to the voiceover.

"And this is the secret hideaway that young Sean Rivers

fled to when he could no longer take the insane pressure of the attention of the world media. To this elite stage school in London, England, where only the very finest talents are allowed access. It was in this magnificent eighteenth century building, where Queen Victoria is said to have once stopped for tea, that Sean chose to hide himself away from the world, desperate to get some respite from the trauma of being so famous so young. But it seems that the relentless pack of journalists have finally tracked him down and are intent on invading his privacy once more. Let's go now to Caridee Columbo who can bring you the latest on the terrible intrusion into Sean's new life from right outside of his school gates."

"Thank you, Linda."

I clapped both of my hands over my mouth as I saw a very blonde, very pink-lipsticked woman holding a C! Celebrity News microphone standing outside the Academy gates. And she wasn't the only reporter there. I could also see a swarm of photographers and journalists with camera crews who looked as if they might be from all over the world.

"Well, Linda, as you can see there is quite an undignified scrum here at the Sylvia Lighthouse Academy for the Performing Arts as the world press try to get a glimpse of young actor Sean Rivers. It was revealed only recently, by his friend and fellow actor, Ruby Parker, that

Sean came here to change his life and try and live out the rest of his childhood in peace. Sean's house was discovered yesterday by tabloid journalists, forcing the poor boy to flee with his mother to the school which is still closed for the holidays. As you can see, Sean doesn't stand much chance of getting that privacy he craves so much any more. All of these people you see behind me want to know only one thing. They want to know the truth behind Sean's dramatic departure from movie-making which broke years worth of contracts worth millions of dollars. Is it true that Oscar-winning director Art Dubrovnik bullied him on the set of soon to be released *The Lost Treasure of King Arthur*? Or could it be, as some of the rumours are saying, that Sean got carried away with the London party lifestyle, even attempting to steal thousands of dollars worth of jewellery when he was under the influence. Some say Sean was trying to escape his cruel and obsessive father, but the very same father, Pat Rivers, says his son was stolen from him by the bitter, mentally unstable and jealous mother who abandoned him as a child. As you know, Linda, much of America thought of Sean as their son and now they want to know – what exactly has happened to him?"

"It's an awful shame that he can't just be left to live his life in peace, isn't it, Caridee?" Linda, the C! announcer, said.

"Yes, it is," Caridee said. "It truly is."

And I thought to myself, *If she really thinks that, then why is she standing outside my school gate doing exactly the same thing as all the other press people? Hounding Sean.*

I pressed the mute button on the remote and buried my head in David's meagre fur. I felt awful, sick inside.

Sean was so happy since he started at the school. Relaxed and acting like any normal fifteen-year-old boy. And now that had been taken away from him, all because of me and my big thoughtless mouth. He would never forgive me. I didn't think that any of my friends would either.

I looked around. Jeremy's house was still mostly silent, sunlight streaming in through the windows, even some birdsong in the garden. I could hear the faint clatter of Augusto in the kitchen and Marie laughing with my mother somewhere. Everything here looked and felt the same, but I knew that on the other side of the world all hell had broken loose for Sean, and it was my fault.

When the phone in the hallway began to ring I knew, I just knew with total certainty, that it was Sean. Even though it would be the middle of the night at home and even though there was no way he could know what I had just seen on C!, I was certain that it had to be him. I scrambled to pick the phone up before one of the adults did.

"Hello?" I said uncertainly into the receiver.

"Oh, hi, is that Ruby?" An unfamiliar female voice spoke in my ear and I breathed out a sigh of relief.

"Yes, speaking," I said.

"Hi, Ruby, it's Suzie Blenheim here – and how are you?"

Suzie Blenheim. My stomach contracted again as I realised that this was it. I was going to find out if I had got the part of Lady Elizabeth. A mixture of emotions churned through my mind because I wasn't ready to get this particular news at this particular moment when I had other things to think about.

At first I thought, *I don't want it, I don't want it any more. I don't deserve it and anyway I need to go home and see Sean and tell him I'm sorry and help make things better again.* And then I thought about how much Sean must hate me at this moment, and if he hated me then Anne-Marie certainly would, and maybe even Nydia and Danny too. Perhaps I'd have to go back to school with everybody hating me and that frightened me. I'd rather live in Hollywood forever than for that to happen.

"Hi Suzie," I said in a small voice. "Do you want to speak to my mum?"

"No." Suzie's voice was warm and friendly. "I think that you should be the first to know, Ruby. We are thrilled to offer you the guest spot of Lady Elizabeth to feature in six episodes of *Hollywood High*!"

There was a long silence during which I knew I was supposed to say something, but nothing came to mind. My swirling mind had suddenly gone blank.

"Ruby?" Suzie repeated my name anxiously.

"I'm sorry... I am just so surprised and... and happy!" The actor part of me finally kicked in and from somewhere I found the joy that should have greeted such fantastic news. "It's wonderful, wonderful news – Mum will be thrilled," I assured her.

"Good," Suzie laughed. "Well, if I may speak to your mother then, please, Ruby. There are a lot of details that need to be ironed out. Details you don't want to worry about, OK? You just think about starting at Beaumont on Monday and we'll see you on set after school. The scripts are on the way to you now."

"OK," I said. I was about to take the phone and go and look for my mum when suddenly I heard her voice on the line. She must have picked up another extension and been listening all the time.

"Suzie, this is great news!" my mother said, and then,

"Put the phone down now, Ruby."

I was happy to oblige. I didn't want to listen to the final details that had to be confirmed. I would be far too busy hiding under the covers of my bed and worrying about what I had done to Sean.

Chapter Ten

The rest of the day dragged by as I nervously waited for my webcam chat with Danny. Then I would really find out what was going on at home.

After Mum had finished talking to Suzie she came and found me in my room under the covers, curled up with David.

"What on earth are you doing under there?" she asked me, pulling the quilt off so that I squinted and squirmed in the sunlight. David yelped and ran off the bed, disappearing through the crack in the door. "Why are you hiding? You're not nervous about starting at Beaumont, are you? Suzie said Adrienne and Nadine are dying to show you off. She thinks you'll have a wonderful time. And as for the part of Lady Elizabeth – well, you could act any of those girls off the screen."

"It's not that," I said. "At least not mainly." I must have looked worried because Mum's brow crinkled just a little and she sat down on the bed.

"What's wrong, Ruby?"

"I'm worried about what's going to happen at home," I told her. She nodded as if she understood completely and for a second I thought that she might already know about Sean.

"You don't have to. I've already spoken to your dad, on the day of the audition, to tell him what we were planning. He was absolutely fine about it. He said that he thought it would be good for you to stay here a bit longer. He thought you'd learn a lot."

"You didn't tell me that you had spoken to Dad!" I said, temporarily forgetting Sean. That piece of news stunned me. I had been waiting for the right moment to call him myself for nearly two weeks and since all the *Hollywood High* stuff had happened, that moment still hadn't come. I had rehearsed how I was going to tell him, deciding that I would make friends with him first, apologise about the way we left things and being rude to his so-called girlfriend. And then I'd tell him about *Hollywood High* and invite him to visit for a few days. Something to make him feel better and included again.

But Mum had cleared it with him and it seemed he wasn't at all bothered if he didn't see me for a few more weeks. In fact, maybe he wasn't bothered if he didn't see me at all. Maybe his life without me had moved on that little bit more, the little bit more that didn't need me in at all.

I looked at Mum, but she didn't have a clue what this all might mean. So I tucked the hurt feeling away in my tummy and tried again to tell her what had happened.

"It's not that," I said. "It's Sean. Sean Rivers."

"Sean?" My mum looked perplexed. "What on earth are you worrying about Sean for?"

I told her what I had seen on C! and she immediately switched on the TV in my room. Sure enough they were repeating the same broadcast.

"Oh dear," Mum said. "But it's not as if you actually said, 'I go to this school and so does Sean Rivers', did you?"

"No, but I said enough to get people thinking, like his dad and about a hundred tabloid journalists. People who were able to track him down through me," I said miserably. "He was so happy and I've ruined it."

"This is bad," Mum said. "We don't want the public to perceive you as the kind of person who would betray a friend!"

"Mum!" I exclaimed. "That's not what I'm worried about. I'm worried about Sean. What can I do to help him? I need to do something!"

Mum looked thoughtful and then patted my hand. "I'll call Sean's mother as soon as she wakes up, if she slept at all with that lot on her trail, poor woman. And I'll talk to Art and Lisa Wells. After all, Art would rather that these bullying rumours were stopped too. I have an idea that might help both your careers."

"I don't want you to help me, I want to help him!" I cried.

"And you will," Mum said firmly. "Now listen, you have to focus on the now. I've changed our air tickets to open returns so that we can fly back any time we like in the next six months. They are being delivered today, so remind me to put them with the passports. And your first script should be here by this afternoon so we'll start to read it through before bed, OK? There's not much time until you start work!"

"I have my web chat with Danny tonight," I reminded her.

"Oh, yes, that," Mum said. "But that will only take a few minutes, won't it?"

"I don't know," I said. And I didn't because I had no idea what Danny was going to say to me.

At the agreed hour I followed the log on instructions Danny had e-mailed me to connect my laptop to his PC. Eventually, a screen came up showing his bedroom at his dad's house and an empty chair, which meant he'd already switched his PC on and was ready. I was nervous. I didn't know if that meant he was eager to see me or to tell me exactly what he thought of me. He was nowhere to be seen though, which made me wonder if he'd changed his mind about talking to me at all. I looked at my watch and thought that I might be a few minutes early so I sat at the desk and stared at Danny's bedroom and waited.

And waited.

"He's decided he doesn't want to see me," I said, looking down at David who was lying at my feet happily chewing the laces of my new trainers. "He's so disgusted with me over Sean that he just doesn't want to know."

"Hi, Ruby, sorry I'm late." Danny's voice suddenly came out of nowhere. I looked up and there he was sitting in his chair. I felt butterflies in my chest. It was good to see him, but he wasn't smiling.

"Been waiting long?" he asked. "I got a bit delayed by a call from the new girl on *Kensington Heights*. Melody. She's asked me to help her rehearse today."

"Oh," I said nervously. "Don't worry about it."

It was hard to tell how Danny was being with me. He looked odd on the laptop screen and somehow he felt further away than when I spoke to him on the phone. But he couldn't have changed that much in two weeks. He was still just my Danny, after all, even if at that precise moment I had grounds to think he might hate me.

"Do you know?" Danny asked me straight out, his voice dark. "About what's going on with Sean?"

"I just found out today. It's all over the news here," I said. "I feel *dreadful*, Danny, I never meant for this to happen. Does Sean hate me?"

I had hoped that Danny was going to tell me not to be so silly, but he didn't.

"He feels pretty bad about it, Ruby," he said. Only his mouth moved a fraction of a second or two after the words came out of the speakers, making them seem all the more stark. "He can't believe that you talked about him at all."

"I didn't *mean* to, I didn't want to," I told him. "I was on TV and there were hot lights and an audience and this guy saying all sorts of awful things about Art and Sean and it just sort of came out – I was trying to stand up for him and Art. Has he seen the interview with Carl Vine? If he did, he'd understand that."

"I don't think he cares how it happened. He's having a bad time of it now – he and his mum had to move out of their house and everything," Danny said with a delayed hand gesture. "You can see why he's feeling pretty gutted, Ruby."

"This isn't how I wanted our webcam chat to be," I said sadly. "You're cross with me too."

"I'm not cross," Danny said. "Just sorry for Sean. I know how hard it can be to keep your life normal when you do what we do and for Sean especially."

"I bet Anne-Marie hates me too," I added.

"She's upset for Sean," Danny said.

"But *you* don't hate me, do you?" I asked, suddenly thinking I could detect a coolness in the detached voice that I was hearing through the speakers.

"No, of course I don't *hate* you," Danny said. "It's just that…"

"Just *what*?" I asked him.

"It seems like you've been away for much longer than two weeks, that's all…"

"What?" I asked. Danny paused, looking down at his desk top. "What do you mean?"

"I… I… dunno, Rube." There was a long pause and I got the feeling Danny was trying to work out how to say something. "I just wish you'd been more careful. It's a bit like appearing on that TV show was more important to you than your mates are."

"I didn't mean it to happen!" I repeated, certain that wasn't what he had really planned to say.

"Yeah, well, it did happen, didn't it, Ruby?" Danny said, and I couldn't be sure because of the webcam, but I thought he was sulking.

Suddenly, I exploded from the pressure of the day and lost my temper.

"Well, fine!" I snapped. "It's fine if you all hate me now because I'm not coming back anyway. I'm starting shooting on *Hollywood High* next week and I'm going to school here so I don't care if you hate me. I'm not coming back."

"Ruby—"

I slammed the laptop lid shut and cut Danny off.

I wasn't completely sure what had just happened, but I had a horrible feeling that Danny and I had just broken up and that I had done it. I opened the laptop up again and tried to get the connection back, but it seemed to have gone, Danny must have turned his PC off. I couldn't guess what he must be thinking of me except that I had turned into a Hollywood diva, the kind of girl he would never want to go out with. But there was something different about him too. I was sure there was something he wasn't telling me.

I didn't know what to do. Should I call him or e-mail him? Or try to talk to Anne-Marie or even Sean? I wanted to, but I was afraid. I knew that they would all blame me for what had happened and I suppose they were right to, because even if I hadn't *meant* it to happen, it had, because I was thoughtless and careless.

Suddenly, I felt so cut off from home, from my friends and Danny and even from Dad, that the prospect of six more weeks in Hollywood brought tears to my eyes. I was helpless. There was nothing I could do to make things better.

All I could do was wait and see what plans Mum, Lisa and Art came up with. And if that worked out and things got back to normal with Sean, then perhaps everything would be all right at home again and maybe Danny would be able to tell me whatever it was he hadn't managed to say on the webcam.

But until then, I just had to get on with things here. I had to throw myself into my new life at Beaumont and my part in *Hollywood High*. I'd have to act like I have never acted before. Because if things didn't get better back at home, then maybe I wouldn't want to leave Hollywood after all.

HOLLYWOOD HIGH©

A BLENHEIM PRODUCTIONS PRODUCTION

SEASON TWO EPISODE 23
'ELIZABETH, THE FIRST'
WRITTEN BY: SUZIE BLENHEIM, JENNY
ROBERTS, SAM JENKINS, HALLE GONZALEZ,
NAVEEN SMITH AND CONNIE KREMER
DIRECTED BY: SUZIE BLENHEIM

SCENE tbc

EXT: DAYTIME, SCHOOL PLAYING FIELDS

LADY ELIZABETH is sitting alone at the
edge of the playing fields watching the
boys take football practice. She looks
vulnerable and alone. HAYDEN keeps
looking over at her, even though he
knows his girlfriend SABRINA is
watching. ELIZABETH is aware he is
watching her and so is SABRINA who is
sitting a little way off with NATALIE,
PARMINDER and LARA. HAYDEN looks over at
SABRINA who is obviously talking about
LADY ELIZABETH behind her back and when

the squad takes a break he trots over to
LADY ELIZABETH.

HAYDEN
(Awkwardly)Hi there, are
you a football fan?

LADY ELIZABETH
(Looks down as if she
might blush, but doesn't)
Who me? I think it looks
very interesting but I
don't really understand
it. In my country football
is something completely
different. This looks more
like rugby to me. My
brothers play rugby, they
are rather good at it. If
I'm honest, I just came
here because it seemed
like a place where I could
sit on my own without
feeling too embarrassed.

HAYDEN glances over at the group of girls who are trying to pretend they are not watching him. SABRINA is looking in a compact, reapplying lip gloss.

                    HAYDEN
          Those girls have been
          giving you a hard time,
          haven't they?

LADY ELIZABETH nods sadly and looks as if she might cry (she doesn't).

                LADY ELIZABETH
          (Voice wobbles slightly) I
          thought at first that we
          could all be friends. I
          don't know what I've done
          to upset them, but they
          aren't talking to me any
          more. It's hard to be a new
          girl at a school in a
          foreign country without any
          real friends.

HAYDEN sighs and looks over again at
SABRINA who is intent on ignoring him. He
seems to come to some decision.

HAYDEN

How about I walk you home
after school? I could tell
you about some of the cool
places to hang out.

LADY ELIZABETH

(Shocked and flustered)
That would be wonderful,
but what about Sabrina?

She glances over at Sabrina who is now
glaring at her with naked fury. HAYDEN
doesn't see it but LADY ELIZABETH smiles
ever so slightly at SABRINA.

LADY ELIZABETH

Won't you get into trouble
with your girlfriend?

HAYDEN

I like Sabrina a lot and we've been dating for a while, but sometimes I don't understand her. I think it's wrong of her to treat you so badly, when you're new. She's just jealous because a lot of the guys think you're cute. Well, let's give her something to be jealous of. When she sees that you and I are just friends and that you're not a threat to her, she'll soon come to her senses.

LADY ELIZABETH

You'd do that for me?

HAYDEN

(Nods) And for Sabrina too. She's a nice person really. It's just that sometimes she forgets it.

HAYDEN goes back to
football practice and LADY
ELIZABETH looks on as
SABRINA marches off,
followed by her friends.
LADY ELIZABETH takes her
cellphone out of her bag
and makes a call.

LADY ELIZABETH
Jenkins? It's me. Please
tell Daddy that I won't be
needing the chauffeur
today. I'm walking home.
(Pauses) Yes Jenkins, me,
walking, it is a miracle
isn't it?

Chapter Eleven

Considering that I am only thirteen, I have had some pretty nerve-wracking moments in my life already.

Having to do my first-ever screen kiss with the boy I used to have the biggest crush on, Justin de Souza, was pretty freaky. Auditioning in front of Art Dubrovnik and Imogene Grant was so frightening that I was actually sick. And next to being almost arrested for grand diamond theft, appearing on national US television in a show that was watched by twenty million people tested my ability to hold on to my last meal quite severely.

But I don't think that I have ever been as scared as I was on my first day at Beaumont, because it wasn't only my first day at a new school, it was my first day at a new foreign school where, as far as I knew, everybody would hate me just as many of the characters in *Hollywood High* hated Lady Elizabeth. And it was also my first day of shooting for some exterior scenes at Beaumont, which *Hollywood High* used for location shoots.

It was also my first day without Danny Harvey being my boyfriend, as far as I could tell, and the first day I could remember when I wasn't sure if Nydia was my best friend any more. I had tried to call her mobile several times since I spoke to Danny, but she never answered. She hadn't replied to my e-mails either. I had half expected that Danny would call me back, or e-mail at least, to try and make things up between us, but he didn't. I didn't hear from him at all which I supposed was all I needed to know about where I stood with him. We were finished. I knew that in my head, but because of the way it happened it just didn't *feel* real.

All I could do right now was get on with the new experiences that the day would bring. But it was hard. I felt like I was doubly alone. With no old friends and no new friends either. And I knew that my character Lady Elizabeth was a scheming, no-good, nasty old cow. But I knew how to act the scenes where she was pretending to be insecure and vulnerable because that was exactly how I felt. It would be the acting confident and in control that would be the difficult bit.

To make matters worse Mum dropped another bombshell just as I was pushing a blueberry pancake around my plate, unable to eat even one bite.

"Great news, Ruby!" she said, smiling at me. Her face had relaxed a lot since her first treatment and although she still looked different with her giant hair and all her make-up, she could at least smile properly now.

"Really?" I asked. I wasn't listening properly. I was more worried about what I was wearing. I wished desperately that Beaumont had a school uniform like Sylvia Lighthouse's Academy did because then, even if you hated it, with its skirt exactly the wrong length and its dreadful grey cardigans that could make even Anne-Marie look frumpy, at least you knew that you *had* to wear it and so did everybody else. Now I had to decide for myself and it was a decision fraught with danger.

How would I know if what I had chosen to wear was anything *like* what a hip American kid would wear? And as I knew that my personal style didn't exactly make me cutting-edge cool back at home, I wasn't feeling too hopeful.

I had carefully studied as many episodes of *Hollywood High* as possible and after several private hours of worrying and trying stuff on, I had decided on my pale blue three-quarter-length trousers (Capri pants they call them here) and pink T-shirt with a pink cardigan. I accessorised with the string of fake pearls Julian had given me and for footwear I chose a pair of trainers decorated with silver stars. I'd brushed my hair a hundred times, which I had read once that Sylvia Lighthouse used to do when she was a girl, and put some sticky, moussey product on it that Julian had left behind to try and smooth it down. I didn't know about make-up. The characters in *Hollywood High* obviously wore make-up, but it wasn't allowed at the Academy. So as Beaumont was a real school and not a soap school, I decided not to put any on.

"Ruby are you listening to me?" my mum said quite sharply. She had a lot less time for my tendency to have my head in the clouds these days.

"Sorry, Mum," I said quietly. "I was worrying about my outfit for school – what do you think?"

"What? Honestly, Ruby, there are more important things to worry about than clothes, you know."

I looked at Mum who was wearing a gold silk shirt over cream trousers with a pair of pale gold, open-toed, high-heeled sandals just to take me to school, and I thought, *If you say so, Mum*. But I didn't say it out loud because Mum obviously thought that what she had to tell me was quite important.

"I spoke to Lisa last night and its great news," Mum told me. "Sean has agreed to fly out to LA with his mother and do an interview to set the record straight.

He's going to do it on *The Carl Vine Show* and the best bit is – you are going to do it with him!"

"Me?" I asked, surprised that Sean would want me anywhere near him.

"Yes, you. It will be perfect," Mum told me happily. "You and Sean can both talk about what it was like to be on the set of *The Lost Treasure of King Arthur*, how wonderful and magical it was and all that business. And you can tell him about the hilarious mistake with the diamonds and how Sean wasn't under the influence of anything at all."

It was the first time I'd heard my mother refer to that night as "hilarious", but recently strange had become normal with Mum so I wasn't surprised any more.

"And you can tell the press that as a child star you understand only too well the pressures of life in the public eye. You and Sean can ask them together to respect Sean's privacy now until he is eighteen, and to pursue him only if he decides to step back into the public eye. It will be brilliant. Brilliant for Sean, brilliant for the film and, best of all, brilliant for you!"

"Did Sean ask for me to do the interview with him?" I asked hopefully.

"No," Mum said. "Lisa arranged it and after some discussion he agreed."

"So he doesn't *want* to see me then?" I asked anxiously. "He's being forced to do the interview with me?"

"No, Ruby, not forced – persuaded." Mum took my plate of untouched food away. "Look, Sean has had a rough time of it and rightly or wrongly he blames you for that. But I'm sure once you see him face to face, you two will be friends again before you know it. And then everything will be back to normal."

"That would be good, Mum," I said wanly. "But somehow I don't think it's going to be that easy."

Mum smiled at me and kissed the top of my head. "Yuck, what have you got in your hair? It tastes revolting!" she exclaimed.

"Gel," I said flatly. "Hair gel or mousse stuff."

"Good," Mum said as she breezed out of the kitchen. "At least you're learning about personal grooming. That's something. Now be by the front door in ten minutes. I've never driven on the right-hand side before and I want to leave in plenty of time!"

Augusto came and sat down next to me and smiled. "Scared about the new school?" he asked. I nodded.

"Scared about the new job?" I nodded.

"Scared about doing an interview with Sean Rivers?" I nodded vigorously several times.

"You're a pretty scared kid right now, aren't you?" Augusto said.

"I'll say," I said in a small voice.

"Well," Augusto shrugged. "There's not much I can do for your fear, Ruby, but if you think a dessert made with more chocolate than you ever thought possible might make you feel better, then I'll make one for you tonight."

I mustered a smile. "Well I've never known chocolate make anything *worse*," I told him. "Thank you, Augusto."

"Things usually work themselves out for the best, you know," Augusto said. "And as long as we always do our best, then we'll never have anything to regret."

It seemed to me just at that moment that I had a lot of things to regret. Probably too many things for a girl of only thirteen. But Augusto was right about one thing. All I could do now was my very best.

I just hoped that it would be enough.

When I picked up my school bag and it barked I knew that something wasn't quite right. I opened the flap and David looked at me from inside with a, "Yeah and what are you going to do about it?" expression.

"Look, David," I said, "I'm really sorry but I don't think you can come to school. I'm fairly sure dogs aren't allowed. But don't worry because when I get back I'll play ball with you in the garden, OK?"

David growled as I attempted to reach in and pull him out.

"He likes you," Jeremy said, appearing behind me, his hands in his pockets.

"Really?" I asked. "Because I always thought it was wagging and licking that were signs of affection in dogs, and not so much the whole biting and growling thing."

"David had been through a rough time when we found him, cut and bruised and terrified," said Jeremy. "I've had him three years now and not once until he met you has he voluntarily been outside the gates of this house. He wants to go where you go which must mean he trusts and likes you. And I'm not surprised – you're a very likeable person, Ruby."

Jeremy bent down and lifted an angry David out of my school bag.

"Am I?" I asked. "I don't feel very likeable at the moment."

"Trust me. Just be yourself and you will never go far wrong," Jeremy said. "Now, run along – your mother's waiting."

It wasn't only Mum who was waiting for me; it was the whole of my future, just waiting for me to mess it all up. Be yourself, Jeremy said. But the question is – who is Ruby Parker?

Right now that question was impossible to answer.

Chapter Twelve

Beaumont was not at all like I had imagined it would be. I thought it would be like all the high schools I have seen in movies. A big old-looking building with a grand entrance, lots of steps leading down to a grassy area where the kids hang out in various groups depending on their popularity status. I suppose that as an actress who knows all too well that what you see on screen is not usually like real life, I shouldn't have been surprised when it was different. But I was. Not because Beaumont didn't look like a movie high school. But because it didn't look like a school at all.

It was an ultra-modern building made from what looked like white steel and glass, so that it dazzled in the sunshine. And it wasn't cube-shaped like most buildings, made up of corners and right angles. It was a series of curves and domes, with white-tiled pathways through large expanses of grass that was so well kept it could almost have been a carpet. As Mum and I followed the signs to the office I noticed that the students at least seemed pretty much as I imagined.

Like Sylvia Lighthouse's Academy for the Performing Arts, this was a stage school and so the pupils were a little more showy and flamboyant than the average kid. (Although, to be fair, I hadn't been to a normal school since I was a very little girl. Maybe normal school kids do ballet in the corridor and sing impromptu musical numbers when they are waiting to go into maths too.) As we walked, I looked closely at what the other girls were wearing and thought that my outfit seemed just about passable. Not that this would help when it came to what I was going to wear tomorrow; I had exhausted my wardrobe getting today's look together.

Mum led me through some arched doors into the school. I had never seen any school that looked so clean and bright. There was no dust, no chipped paint and no faint smell of disinfectant. It was like walking on board a space ship.

We came to the school office and after knocking Mum pushed the door open. A woman with auburn hair, who was studying a laptop, looked up and smiled at us.

"Hello there," Mum said. "This is my daughter, Ruby Parker. She's enrolling here today."

"Oh, yes, hi." The woman erupted into a friendly smile and held out her hand to shake. "It's a pleasure to have you with us for a spell, Ruby," she told me with a warm and slightly husky voice. "My name is Marianne Green, I'm the School Principal so if there is any help you need with anything, with where your next class is or how your curriculum is working out, then I'm the lady to come to. I've been in touch with your school and spoken at length to your form teacher, Miss Greenstreet. What a lovely lady! We've worked out a programme of learning for you. You'll attend the appropriate classes for your year group so you can get a real feel for what it's like to go to school here, you'll get special assignments for you to do at home, to make sure you keep up with your classes in England. We'll Fedex that work back to Miss Greenstreet, so it will be graded and count towards your exams. Does that sound good?"

"Great," I said, a little overwhelmed by all the information. Homework. No matter where you go in the world there is always homework.

"Your first class this morning is English. We're all expecting you to be an expert on that!" Ms Green and my mum laughed. "If you want to go, Mrs Parker, I'll show Ruby where to go."

"Super," Mum said. She turned to me and put a hand

on either shoulder. "Now, try not to be nervous and have a great day. I'll be there to pick you up after you've finished shooting this afternoon, OK?"

I nodded, resisting the urge to throw my arms round my mum and wail like a five-year-old.

"That's my girl," she said, dropping a quick kiss on my forehead and screwing her mouth up as she tasted my hair gel once again. I heard her heels clicking down the corridor without even pausing once.

"Well then, Ruby," Ms Green said with a smile. "Follow me."

As soon as I walked into the class I was engulfed.

"Ruby!" Nadine squealed, hugging me tightly.

"It's so cool you're here!" Adrienne exclaimed, leading me to a desk by the window across an aisle from them.

"We saved you this seat, so you'd be next to us," Nadine said.

"Thanks!" I said, feeling enormous relief at finding two friendly faces waiting for me. Everyone was looking at me with open curiosity. There was one girl with dark brown hair sitting at the back who sort of glowered, but almost everybody else seemed very nice.

"This is Carrie, Lauren and Maya." Nadine introduced me to three more girls, two of whom, Lauren and Maya, I recognised from *Hollywood High*.

"Hello," I said. "Pleased to meet you."

"This is Jack and Cory, and *this*..." Adrienne smiled and before I knew it she had her arms around the shoulders of the real-life person who played her screen boyfriend. "...is my boyfriend, Hunter Blake."

"Hunkily Handsome Hunter Blake" as *Teen Girl! Magazine* would no doubt describe him one day.

"Oh – h-hi... hello," I said and I felt my cheeks burn. It was embarrassing on so many levels. First, because here I was face to face with a seriously good-looking boy, who in normal circumstances I would have Blu-tacked to my wall in poster form a few weeks from now. Second, because he was clearly going out with Adrienne and by blushing I had made it perfectly clear that I thought her boyfriend was cute, which I think is universally considered to be quite bad form. And third, because *everybody* saw it happen.

"Oh, Ruby, you are so blushing!" Maya giggled.

"No, she's *not*," Nadine said. "It's hot and that pink top is reflecting off of her skin. But even if she was, who'd blame her with all of you staring? Give the girl a chance to sit down and relax!"

I smiled gratefully at Nadine and nodded another safer silent hello to Hunter. He was taller than the other boys, with friendly blue eyes and dark brown hair that flopped down over them. Exactly the kind of boy that any normal girl with a pulse would feel slightly wibbly about meeting.

It was something I would have to get over though as I had a lot of scenes with Hunter Blake. In fact, Lady Elizabeth did her very best to steal his character, Hayden, from Sabrina. If I didn't get this blushing under control, I was fairly sure I'd spend the entire time I was here bright red. And Nadine was right about one thing. It didn't go with my pink top.

"You are so right to stay out of the sun," Nadine went on. "The sun is so the worst thing for wrinkles. If you like, though, I can give you the name of a really good tan artist? She does Lindsay Lohan."

"Thanks, Nadine," I said as I slid into my seat. "But Suzie told me not to tan. She wants me pale and English rose-like, I suppose."

"Pale is totally in," Adrienne said. "You just have to look at your friend Imogene…"

But before she could finish talking the teacher came in. She was quite young, the same sort of age as Miss Greenstreet. But whereas Miss Greenstreet was all sort of warm and cuddly and easily distracted if you asked her an entirely unrelated question (like what kind of wedding dress she would have if she ever got married or if she thought tulips were nicer than daffodils), this teacher looked, well… focused.

The complete silence that fell the moment she entered the room seemed to back up that theory.

"Good morning, class," she said, her voice as clear and as sharp as glass. "And good morning to our new student, Ruby Parker. Please stand up, Ruby."

Mortified, I did.

"Hello, Ruby. I am Ms Martinez and I will be teaching you English. I hope you enjoy your time here."

"Yes, miss, thank you, I will," I said. It felt a little bit like she was ordering me to have a good time rather than asking me.

"Good. As you're on your feet, you can start us off. I've picked a book to make you feel at home. *Jane Eyre*. Read from the first paragraph, please, Ruby, and then tell us why this book changed the face of English literature as we know it."

The day went very quickly. Partly because it finished just after lunch and partly because with Nadine and Adrienne fussing around me constantly, I didn't have time to be nervous. They showed me where to sit at break time, what to eat in the canteen, told me who was who in the pecking order of the school and who was not really anyone at all. I realised quickly that by knowing them I had an automatic in with the in-crowd and they were sort of the Jade Caruso and Menakshi Shah of Beaumont. And considering I was me, not renowned for being the most naturally popular of girls, I realised I was very lucky. Unlike some.

"That's Tina Petrelli," Adrienne said, pointing openly at the girl in brown who was sitting at a table alone during break. "She looks like somebody died because we told her to move so you could sit by us in class. Why she thought she could be anywhere near us is a mystery! The back of the class is the only place for someone like that – where nobody has to see her hideous face!" She and Nadine giggled.

And so did I.

"No one knows what she's even *doing* at Beaumont," Nadine added, her voice sharp. "This is a school for the stars of the future, it says so in the curriculum. Look at her, Ruby – can *you* see any star quality?"

I looked over at Tina who was staring deeply into her yoghurt. I thought that she must know that we were talking about her. She could probably feel our eyes on her and hear the tones of our voices even if she couldn't make out the words. I thought about Nydia who used to get teased so much because of her weight and still did, even though she was gradually losing it. And I thought about me, so often the butt of people's jokes at school. I had got into my fair share of scrapes and arguments with other girls, thrown a few names back at boys who were teasing me. But I had never, ever picked on anybody just because they were different, just because they didn't fit in. But here I was on my first day, thousands of miles away from home, and at that moment Adrienne and Nadine were the only friends I had in the whole wide world. I needed them.

"She looks about as talented as a slug," I said, setting the pair off into peels of giggles.

"A slug!" Adrienne called out, loud enough for Tina to look up. "Tina the talented slug – good one, Ruby."

I felt sick inside, horrible and disgusted with myself. But I didn't stop them. I just laughed along too.

"Oh, look, there's Zach Patel," Adrienne whispered, nodding towards a boy who was walking across the cafeteria towards Hunter's group. "He's cute, don't you think?"

I looked at the boy they were talking about. He was tall and lanky with a nice friendly smile.

"You couldn't call him un-cute," I said, which I was pleased to find made the girls laugh again.

"I know," Nadine said, leaning closer. "And guess what? *That's* who we've decided is going to take you to the Valentine's dance."

"Pardon?" I said, looking back at Zach laughing with his friends. "Does he know?"

"He will," Adrienne explained. "After we've styled you a bit more, taken you shopping a few times, turned you into one of us, then we're going to introduce you to Zach properly. Don't worry, we'll tell you how to act and what to say, and we'll get him to ask you to the dance even though he thinks he wants to ask Lisa Caldwell. We always get what we want."

"Best of all, when he asks you and not Lisa Caldwell, she will actually *die*," Nadine added.

"Do we hate her?" I asked. "Why?"

Adrienne's razor-sharp glare cut across the room as she got a girl who I assumed was Lisa Caldwell in her sights. "Just *look* at the dumb moose."

I looked across the room and thought that Lisa looked perfectly OK to me. Pretty with glossy curly hair and quite a few friends around her. If I was Zach Patel, I'd ask Lisa to the dance over me any time. She looked really nice, even saying "hi" to Tina as she left, instead of hurling a hurtful comment like Adrienne had done.

"Well, of course, you two know what's best," I said. "It's just that—"

"I know!" Nadine interrupted me. "You're going to say you have a boyfriend at home and it would be wrong to go to the dance with another guy."

I hadn't been about to say that actually. I had been about to say that surely Zach would only ask the girl he really liked to the dance, not the girl that Adrienne and Nadine thought he should ask. But Nadine's comment reminded me with a sharp pang that I had broken up with Danny.

"Actually, I broke up with my boyfriend," I said a little sadly, glad at last for the chance to talk about it. "I don't know what happened. One minute we were talking and then—"

"Perfect!" Adrienne squealed. "This is going to be great. Now you can steal Zach away from Lisa without having to feel bad about it!"

"Right," I said hesitantly. "Yay."

"Hey," Nadine lowered her voice and leaned in further, "is it true that you dated Sean Rivers and he dumped you for some English model so you outed him from his secret hideaway as revenge?"

"No!" I said so loudly that a few other kids looked over to where we were sitting. "No, we were never going out. For a while the press at home and everyone thought we were, but that was a mix-up. It was quite funny actually—"

"What's he like?" Adrienne asked me. "Is he as cute in real life as he is in *The Underdogs*? Is he a good kisser? I bet he's a *really* good kisser!" She and Nadine cackled away.

"I wouldn't know," I said firmly. "I haven't kissed him properly and I didn't mean to give away where he was living – it was an accident."

"So what's going to happen to Sean now?" Adrienne asked me intently, putting me on my guard. "If anyone knows it's you, right? And do you know how cool dishing dirt like that will make us? Spill, Ruby."

There was something about Adrienne that made you want to do exactly what she told you. I was about to tell her when I remembered why I was in such a mess with my friends back home and had possibly lost Sean and even Danny forever. Mum had told me that plans for Sean's exclusive interview were top secret. I didn't want to make the mistake of giving away any more secrets about Sean, especially not to Adrienne who I got the feeling only used her superpowers for evil.

"I don't know," I shrugged. Adrienne squinted at me. "Honestly, why would I know? No one tells me anything."

Considering that I am terrible at lying, they seemed to believe me. I decided not to think about what would happened once they found out the truth.

"Well, I want *you* to make up with him so that when he comes back to Hollywood *you* can introduce him to me and *we* will fall instantly in love," Adrienne said happily as if her wish really was my command.

"But what about Hunter?" I asked her, a little shocked.

"Hunter is the male lead in *Hollywood High*," Adrienne said with a shrug. "And he's the best-looking boy in our grade, so naturally I'm dating him. But if Sean Rivers were available? Well, *that* would be a whole other story…"

"Okey-dokey," I said, even though I didn't think it. I felt a bit like I was being swept away in a fast-flowing river of crazed girl power.

"Working with you is going to be so great, Ruby," Nadine said, her voice suddenly warm and friendly again.

"Thanks," I said with a smile, feeling my knotted tummy muscles relax a little. No matter how different or difficult it was to be friends with these girls, at least I could feel good about the fact that they had chosen to like me for me.

"Hey," Adrienne said suddenly, "when you go to the premiere of your movie you can take us as your guests and we can all get photographed on the red carpet – how cool will that be?"

"That will be cool," I said. Perhaps they didn't like me for me after all. But they *liked* me, and even if it was just because of the people I knew or a potential invitation to a film premiere, as far as I could see it was *much* safer to be liked than hated by them. And that was the way I intended it to stay.

When it came to shooting my first scenes for *Hollywood High,* it was actually quite relaxing compared to hanging out with Nadine and Adrienne, trying to think up mean and funny things to say about whomever they decided to pick on at any given moment. I noticed that all the people at the beginning of the day who'd said "hi" and smiled at me had gradually begun to ignore me until only the inner circles of girls that Nadine and Adrienne approved of would even look at me.

So, despite my blushing issue, it was actually a relief that all of my first scenes were with Hunter Blake, shot on location outside the school. I didn't know him at all apart from the article in *It's Your Life!* called 'Get to know Hunter Blake – his Top Ten Favourite Things', so at least I knew his favourite colour was green and he seemed like a really nice, easy-going boy who reminded me a bit of Sean, except that he made me blush and Sean never did.

"Hey, Ruby," he said while we were waiting for Suzie to come and listen to us read our scenes through together. "How was your first day at Beaumont? Have Adi and Nadine managed to clone you into one of them yet?"

I laughed properly for the first time that day. "They're still working on it," I said with a smile, shading my eyes from the sun as I looked up at him. "They've been really kind to me. My first day would have been really scary if it hadn't been for them."

"That's true," Hunter said, mimicking the deep and gravelly tone of a film trailer voiceover. "*They have the power to make your day really great or really, really bad.*"

"I know which I prefer," I told him.

"Me too," Hunter said with a rueful grin. Then I saw Adrienne watching us from a distance and even though I wasn't standing at all close to Hunter, I took a step back.

"Hey, guys," Suzie Blenheim came over. "Let me hear you read the scene through while they set up the cameras and the lighting." She smiled at me. "We don't like to rehearse too much, Ruby; we like to keep that realistic, improvised edge. If you want to change the script a little or if you have any ideas for the scene, then tell us. We're all very open here, OK?"

I nodded and felt a bubble of excitement in my tummy. After all, this is what I loved to do. The reason I spent so many years on *Kensington Heights*, why I made myself sick auditioning for *The Lost Treasure of King Arthur* and why, despite all of my reservations, I was here today, was to act.

Acting was the fun part, the wonderful and magical part that made me feel happy and alive. And if I could forget, even just for a little while all of the complicated and difficult parts that seemed to come with it, then it would be worth it.

When Hunter and I read through the scene I was a different girl in a different world for a few minutes, and it felt good.

"That was great, Ruby," Suzie told me with a broad smile once we had finished. "But I need you to relax a little and remember Lady Elizabeth wants to take Hayden from his girlfriend. So you need to try *acting* shy and vulnerable, but sort of flirtatious and confident too. Can you do that?"

I looked at her. "Yes," I said, thinking to myself that if I could, it would be a first in both my acting and my real life.

But here I was on the set of a TV show, acting opposite one of America's hottest young stars. All I had to do was to let myself disappear into the mind of Lady Elizabeth. Instead of being Ruby saying her words, I had to *be* Elizabeth, I had to *think* and *feel* her words. And gradually, after take after take, that special kind of magic you sometimes get when you are acting really well began to happen.

"That's a wrap for today, everybody!" Suzie called a few hours later to a ripple of applause from the cast and crew. "Really great work, guys," she said, coming over to me and Hunter and giving us both a hug. "Ruby, you nailed it, honey. There's a day off for you kids tomorrow and then interior scenes on Wednesday and Friday. And pick-ups Saturday morning. Good job, everyone!"

I walked back to the make-up and costume trailers where I found Jeremy talking to Mr Blenheim.

"Any time we can persuade you to do a guest role, you let me know," Mr Blenheim was telling Jeremy. "We love to get quality actors like you on board. It would light the whole show up. Give it kudos."

"Thank you. I'll bear it in mind," Jeremy said politely, smiling as he saw me approaching. I said hello and goodbye to Mr Blenheim as he left to talk to Suzie.

"So, Ruby, how was your day of firsts?" Jeremy asked me jovially.

"Fine," I said happily. "Great actually, especially the scenes I shot today. I remembered what you taught me." I looked around. "Where's Mum. She said she'd be here."

"Janice couldn't make it," Jeremy said. "A meeting came up at the last minute. She's with Lisa planning what you and..." He glanced around at the group gathering around us, Adrienne pushing her way to the front. "Well, it was important, Ruby."

"Oh," I said. I felt disappointed. I was looking forward to being with Mum on the drive home, me telling her about my day and listening to her stories. And then maybe we'd sing along to our favourite new song and Mum would get all the words wrong. I wanted to tell her about Adrienne and Nadine and maybe, if she seemed in an understanding mood, even about the girl called Tina who I had been unkind to. I wanted her to tell me that I was wrong to do that, because although I already knew that, knowing didn't seem enough to stop me doing it.

"She sends her apologies," Jeremy said. "And as I didn't have scenes to shoot this afternoon, I came to pick you up instead of just sending the chauffeur."

"That is nice," I told him, smiling and feeling suddenly very tired. "Thank you."

I glanced around at Adrienne, Nadine and quite a few of the other cast members who were all waiting to meet Jeremy Fort.

"Well," I said. "Let me introduce you to my new friends."

Later that night, after two helpings of chocolate pudding, I climbed gratefully into bed, with David curled up in a tiny bony ball at my feet. I was exhausted and the thought of getting up and going through another whole school day made me feel even more tired. It was something I had to get used to though, because I would be doing it every weekday for the next six weeks. I was supposed to have been back in England, but now it wouldn't be until late February that I'd get back home. I wondered if Everest would even talk to me because he was bound to know I'd been hanging out with a dog. And not even a proper dog, but the silliest, smallest and crossest dog the world had ever known.

Tomorrow was going to be hard. Not only because I only had one acceptable thing to wear (which now had chocolate sauce down it), or because my new friends frightened me most of the time. It would also be hard because, despite everything, I was homesick.

Not just for the grey skies and wet pavements, a yearning of Jeremy's that I suddenly understood. Not just for the buildings, my house, my bedroom and my cat. And not only for the people that I missed so much, Dad and Nydia, Danny and the others.

I was homesick for a home that I was sure had vanished.

A dad who didn't seem to care about me any more, friends who hated me and an ex-boyfriend who was probably already dating Jade Caruso.

I felt like I was homesick with no real home to go to.

22 Green Park Road
London NW1

Dear Ruby,

I hope you don't mind me writing to you.
I thought about sending an e-mail, but it
didn't seem right. I thought about phoning
too, but I knew if I talked to you I
wouldn't get what I wanted to say clear
in my mind.

I'm sorry that when we spoke on the
webcam I was funny with you and you got
upset. Rubes, I know you never meant
to spoil things for Sean and everything
that happened was just you being on TV
in America and not realising what you
were saying. I saw a tape of you on
that show and it was odd. It made me
think that you weren't my Ruby Parker
any more; you were Ruby Parker,
Hollywood Star. Which made me think,
who am I now? Am I the same Danny
Harvey that kissed you on the set of

199

Kensington Heights? I don't think I am any more, which probably sounds strange because you've only been gone three weeks, but it's been long enough for some things to happen.

Ruby, I think we should break up. You always told me that we are too young to act like Romeo and Juliet and get all serious, and I think you are right.

You are a good friend and I still really like you. I hope that when you are back we will be OK as friends.

Take care then,
Danny

Chapter Thirteen

Danny's letter came on the Saturday after I had finished my first week on *Hollywood High*. It was waiting for me on a silver plate on the table by the door.

When I saw his handwriting my heart leapt a little bit. I ran up the stairs with David at my heels and took the letter straight to my bedroom to read, full of happiness to have heard from him.

My first ever love letter, I thought, as I sat on my bed and opened the envelope imagining all the sweet and lovely things that Danny would say to me and how sorry he was and how much he missed me.

I was disappointed.

I didn't expect to cry, but I did. Suddenly, as the words he had written sank in and I realised that we were actually properly finished, for good. As the tears came and I lay down on my bed, buried my head in the pillow and wept, David's cold and wet pointed muzzle poked me in the cheek as he licked away the salty tears.

"Ruby?" I heard Mum's voice on the other side of the door. "Ruby are you coming down for lunch?"

I held my breath and waited for all trace of tears to be gone from my voice. I didn't want Mum to catch me crying.

"In a minute," I said when I thought I sounded normal again. Obviously, I didn't sound normal enough because Mum opened the door and came in, setting David off into a barking frenzy.

"Oh, shut up, you idiot dog," my mum said, sending him scooting under the covers with a whimper.

"Ruby, why are you crying?" she asked me in a much softer voice that made me want to cry even more, because Mum had not been very mum-like recently and I had missed her fussing over me more than I thought possible.

She sat on the edge of the bed and put the palm of her hand on my back. I pointed at the letter that had slid on to the floor and tried to speak, but my words got all muddled up in sobs. Mum picked up the letter.

"May I read it?" she asked. I nodded.

"Oh dear, Ruby," Mum said when she put down the letter. "I'm sorry about that. I thought Danny was a nice boy, I really did, and you two were sweet together. But you know, you *are* only thirteen. And you two do live on opposite sides of the world now."

"No, we don't!" I protested. "This is only meant to be a holiday! He says that I'm different, but I'm not. *He* is. He's changed and something else apart from his Christmas number one and six thousand Christmas cards has done it to him. And we're not living here *forever.*"

"Well, who knows where events might take us," Mum said lightly. "Look, darling, I know you feel bad, but I promise you in a few weeks you won't even remember what you saw in him. In a few years you won't even remember who he was."

"I will!" I answered. "Just because I'm a kid doesn't mean I don't feel things!"

"I know you feel lots of things, but what I'm saying is that they will pass," Mum said.

I lay still for a moment and looked at the pattern on my pillowcase. There was something *I* had to know.

"Mum." I sat up and rubbed my eyes, smudging the mascara I'd so carefully applied earlier, practising to get perfect. "Can I ask you something?"

Mum nodded and smiled.

"If I tell you that I want to go home, for good, will you promise to take me?"

Mum looked at me levelly. "Do you want to go home now?" she asked me instead of answering the question.

I thought about what it would be like seeing Danny and Nydia and the others when I wasn't friends with them and it made me want to cry again. I swallowed the tears though.

"No, not right now. But if I *do* want to go home, even if I get offered loads of roles here and get nominated for an Oscar, will you just take me without trying to make me stay?"

Mum nodded. "If that's what you really want, then I will," she said. "But hopefully, it won't come to that." She gave me a quick hug and kissed the top of my head.

"Now wash your face and come down for lunch. I've just spoken to Suzie and she says they are really pleased with how you are doing. Also I have lots to tell you about the release of *The Lost Treasure of King Arthur*, including the premiere, so start thinking about what to wear!"

A lot of the things Mum said to me as I picked at lunch washed over my head. I vaguely heard something about a premiere, some interviews and possibly even a photo shoot for some magazine. And then I heard Sean's name.

"Say that again?" I asked her.

"Sean is arriving here next Friday, in time for the release of the film. He'll escort you to the premiere. But before that, he and you will record an interview for *The*

Carl Vine Show, all taped beforehand with no audience so much less pressure for you.

"Sean's coming in a week?" I asked. "And he's taking me to the premiere? But that means photographers and press and that is exactly what he doesn't want."

"Apparently Art has talked to him about how the film is being received by the critics and how important it is that he supports it. So, being an honourable young man, Sean has agreed to do this one last bit of publicity before retiring for good."

"Poor Sean," I said, staring at my tuna salad.

"Well I'm sure there are millions of fifteen-year-old boys who would love to be famous movie stars so I don't think we'll feel too sorry for Sean."

I looked at my mum in surprise. "Millions of boys might want it, but until you've done it you don't know how hard it is," I told her. "And it was harder for Sean than anyone."

"Well," my mum said. "Maybe. Now eat up all that baby spinach leaf. You've got a busy week ahead and you'll need all of your strength."

It's Your Life!

The magazine for girls that have really got it going on

GET TO KNOW... RUBY PARKER!

This week we're getting to know the latest export from Cool Britannia – Ruby Parker!

IYL: If you could be a pet, which type of pet would you be?
RP: I'd be my cat Everest, because he has the best life of any cat I know. All he does is lay in the sun all day or on a radiator and eat food.

IYL: And who would you most like to feed you kitty treats?
RP: Oh, I don't know! Someone nice.

IYL: If you were a cookie, what type of cookie would you be?
RP: Easy. A double chocolate chip cookie.

IYL: Which is better, a night in with a movie and the boy you have a crush on, or a night out with your girlfriends dancing till dawn!
RP: My mum wouldn't like me to stay out until dawn, but I'll pick dancing all night.

IYL: Describe your personality in three words.
RP: Gosh, um, fun, friendly and fashionable!

So there you have it! Now you know Ruby Parker better than she knows herself!

Mum was right about my busy week. It was a week of being an actual celebrity, of being someone who wasn't famous for her acting (because no one in America had even seen me act yet). But just famous for being… well, famous.

First of all, Adrienne and Nadine nearly went into hyperspace when I told them that Sean would be escorting me to the premiere of *The Lost Treasure of King Arthur* and that Wide Open Universe had invited all of the cast and crew of *Hollywood High* to it too.

"Sean Rivers is taking us to the premiere!" Adrienne had shrieked at the top of her voice.

"Well, me, technically," I replied hesitantly, but then I saw that scary look in her eye and added, "But of course he'll be with all of us."

And from that point on it got kind of embarrassing because the three of us (but mainly the two of them) never stopped talking about Sean and how wonderful it would be to meet him, and how he'd asked especially to meet Adrienne (I didn't remember that bit, but I thought it was best not to contradict) and what we (they) were going to say, wear, think and do with Sean. Oh, and by the way, wasn't it wonderful that Sean Rivers would only come out of hiding for Adrienne (me) and no one else?

If Adrienne and Nadine didn't get sick of the sound of their own voices then everyone else certainly did. The students who weren't on Adrienne's elite list of friends might have avoided me before, but now it was clear that they hated me. And I didn't really blame them. It must have looked as though I was properly stuck up and that I considered myself to be too good for anyone else. The truth wasn't like that at all, but Nadine and Adrienne had sort of taken me over. They told me how to look, what to say and how to act, and I let them. Without their help I would have been completely lost and stuck out on the edge of school society, which was somewhere I didn't want to be, especially not in Hollywood.

Besides, Adrienne could be funny even if she could be mean, and when I hung out with her I also got to hang out with Hunter. He still made me blush whenever he talked to me, but he made me forget about how much I missed Danny, and he knew how to make me laugh properly, and not just because I was too frightened not to.

One morning recess I discovered to my surprise that not all of the kids Adrienne hated, automatically hated me back. I was waiting outside the girls' loo for Adrienne to finish her make-up before we were picked up and taken to the studio to film some scenes (where they would take off all that make-up and put some different stuff on) when Tina Petrelli went by. She walked a step or two past me, then stopped, turned around and said, "Hey, Ruby."

"Oh!" I checked over my shoulder to make sure she wasn't greeting someone else. "Um, hello," I said with a smile. Tina hadn't even looked at me since my first day when I had taken her desk.

"I just wanted to say that I love you in *Kensington Heights*. I watch it on BBC America. When you play Angel you get right under her skin. It was real deep. Not that glossy, shallow garbage they do on *Hollywood High*."

"Oh, don't you like it?" I asked her, surprised.

"Nobody cool likes it," she told me with a shrug. "It's for dorks."

"It's very popular in the ratings," I said.

"Well, that goes to show there are a lot of dorks out there," Tina said with a chuckle. When she smiled she looked like a different person; her face opened up and her bright brown eyes sparkled. She looked friendly, fun and although not exactly fashionable (my three stupid words from the 'Get to know Ruby Parker' article), just the kind of girl I'd enjoy hanging out with.

"*Kensington Heights* seems like a long time ago," I said, even though it was only a few months since I had left the show.

"Your life *has* changed a lot recently," Tina said sympathetically. "Are you happy, Ruby?"

I paused for a moment, surprised by a question that nobody else had asked me.

"Well," I said, "I'm doing what I've always dreamed of doing, but then again I suppose I was doing that before and back at home it seemed a whole lot less frightening..."

"So are you happy?" Tina pressed me for an answer.

"Acting makes me happy," I replied. "But sometimes all the stuff that goes with it is hard to deal with."

"Ah, yes," Tina nodded sagely. "The trappings of fame."

We smiled at each other.

"I'm in a theatre club," Tina said. "I know its a bit obvious to be in a theatre club in a dramatic arts school, but some of us have devoted ourselves to theatre as an art form because we feel it's more relevant to what acting is truly about."

"Sounds interesting," I said, and I meant it because although I'd done a lot of TV and even film in my short career, I'd never done any theatre. Not even a school play.

"If you're really interested, we're putting on a production of *The Seagull*. Do you know it?"

I shook my head slowly, feeling a little bit stupid.

"You'd love it," Tina assured me. She hesitated again, biting at her bottom lip. "Look, if you can get away from the witches, why don't you come one day after school and see what you think?"

"The witches?" I bit my lip but smiled. It was a pretty good description of what Adrienne and Nadine could be like, cackling and plotting all the time. "Well…"

But before I could answer, the loo door swung open and Adrienne appeared, fully made-up and ready to face having her make-up redone.

"Why are you hanging around?" she snapped at Tina sharply, looming over her in her heeled shoes. "Ruby doesn't talk to you. She doesn't even look at you, OK?"

Tina didn't move. She looked at me, her eyebrows raised in a question. "What do you say, Ruby?" she asked.

Adrienne narrowed her eyes at me.

I wanted to say that I would go to Tina's theatre club because it sounded interesting and fun, and if I hung out with Tina, I might not be nervous and frightened of saying something wrong all the time. There was a chance, I thought, that if I said yes to Tina, Adrienne would be surprised but not offended and might even start to treat her a bit better. *Or* she could despise me and make my life for the rest of my stay at Beaumont a misery too.

I just didn't feel brave enough to find out which.

"I don't think so," I said, unable to look Tina in the eye.

"I was so wrong about you," Tina said in disgust. "You're no better than they are."

"You dream about being like me," Adrienne called out after her. "I have nightmares about waking up like you!" She swung an arm around my shoulder and led me off to find Nadine and Hunter and the others.

"I don't know how she had the nerve to talk to you. Loser!"

I am ashamed to say that I didn't disagree.

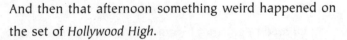

And then that afternoon something weird happened on the set of *Hollywood High*.

We were filming a fight scene set in the canteen. It was going to be a food fight started by Lady Elizabeth to try and make Sabrina look bad in front of Hayden. We'd been rehearsing it with bits of screwed-up coloured paper, each a different colour for a different type of food, and in one shot Adrienne and I had even had to have stunt doubles because the studio wasn't insured for what injuries some chocolate cake in the face might cause us when travelling at speed.

I was excited about shooting it because throwing food at Adrienne could never be anything but fun, and apart from that it would take my mind off the things I couldn't stop thinking about, like Danny's letter and Sean's arrival.

We'd done the first couple of takes which were really funny, and then we had to break while our stunt doubles took our places. (They put a wig and a school uniform on two very tough looking ladies who chewed gum and had scars.) Adrienne was having her yoghurt-caked hair restyled so I thought I'd get a glass of water from craft services (which is what they call the refreshments area on set).

I was standing, all covered in jelly and yoghurt, when this man in a pair of overalls who looked like he might be one of the lighting crew came over to me.

"How are you today, Miss Parker?" he asked, pouring himself a glass of water.

"Fine!" I said with a laugh, gesturing down at my food-covered self.

"Looking forward to the premiere of your film next week?"

"Um, yes, thanks," I said, a little bit surprised because none of the other crew had ever asked me anything like that. Usually they just told me to get out of the way and stop talking during takes. I looked around. Everyone else, including most of the crew, was busy watching the stuntwomen throw each other across a table laden with food. I wanted to watch it too.

"Well, must get on," I said cheerfully, finishing my drink. "Bye!"

The man stepped in front of me. He was smiling, but suddenly I felt uneasy.

"It'll be nice for you to see Sean Rivers again, won't it?" the man asked me.

I hesitated. I didn't want to seem rude, especially not to a crew member, because Jeremy always said it was important not to act as if you were a superstar on set, because no one was anybody without the support of the technicians. And apart from that he was a grown-up and I was a kid. Mum was always telling me to respect my elders and not be rude to adults. All the same, I wondered what on earth he, a lighting man, was asking me those kinds of questions for.

"Well, yes, Sean's a good friend," I said with a shrug. A cheer went up from the crowd around the set as Fake Adrienne landed head first on a crash mat.

"So it's not true that he's cut you off because of your betrayal and is only making an appearance on *The Carl Vine Show* because he's been bullied into it by Art Dubrovnik? Are you saying he *doesn't* hate you for ruining his life?"

I stared at the man. No one was supposed to know about the Carl Vine interview yet. Suddenly, I realised what was wrong. This wasn't a lighting man. This was a journalist who had sneaked on set to find me, deliberately to try and catch me out and make me say something about Sean.

"Leave me alone!" I shouted at him as loudly as I possibly could, thinking about the personal safety classes we'd had at the Academy one term. "GET AWAY FROM ME!"

I was aware of people running towards us, but in the seconds before they could arrive the man took a camera out of his pocket and a flash went off in my face, dazzling me.

"Thanks for the interview, Ruby," he said with a laugh, before running off into the maze of sets and corridors that ran through the studio. The security guards chased him, but later Suzie said he must have known someone on the inside because he'd got out through an alarmed fire door – and the alarm had not gone off.

"Are you OK, Ruby?" Hunter asked. I had sat down with a cup of tea, yoghurt drying in my hair. I was shaking; I couldn't believe that someone had posed as a lighting engineer just to catch *me* out and try and make *me* say something he could use to upset Sean even more.

"Not really," I admitted. Hunter sat down beside me and put his arm around me, which didn't do much for my shakes, but did make me feel better.

"Don't stress it, Ruby," Adrienne said. "That kind of thing happens all the time. Actually you should think of it as kinda cool. They never pap B-listers. It means you've arrived!" She sighed and rolled her eyes. "I wish he'd approached me, I'd have given him a quote about Sean." She caught Hunter's look. "To protect Ruby of course. Poor Ruby."

Suzie Blenheim came and knelt down in front of me. "I've called your mom and she's on her way over. I know it was a shock and I'm really sorry that it happened to you here at work. We'll find out how, I promise you. We take our security very seriously here, especially when there are minors being put at risk. When we find out who let that guy in we will fire them." Suzie held my hands in hers and didn't seem to mind their congealed stickiness. "Look Ruby, I hate to ask you, but do you think you can finish the scene? I know you're feeling pretty wobbly, but if you can carry on that would be just great."

The food fight had lost all of its fun, but I wasn't here to have fun. This was work, work they were paying me quite a lot of money to do. I *had* to get up and get on with it no matter how shaky I felt. The show had to go on. Brett Summers, Jeremy Fort and even Imogene Grant would have said the same if they were in this situation.

"Yes, of course," I said to Suzie. "I'm fine to finish the shoot."

"Great!" Suzie said, dropping my hands. "Make-up! We need to freshen that yoghurt!"

But not even shoving Adrienne's face into a vat of custard could shake the feeling of fear and uncertainty that the journalist's questions had started in me. It was bad enough that he had asked them. But what if…?

What if what he had said about Sean hating me *was* true?

By Wednesday Adrienne had formally launched plan "Get Zach to Take Ruby to the Dance Instead of Lisa". Which involved me sitting with Adrienne, Nadine, Hunter and Zach for lunch. I had no idea how me saying nothing and laughing at everything Zach said even if it wasn't funny (which it mostly wasn't) was going to get him to take me to the dance. I didn't even *want* to go the dance with him, or anyone especially, not after what had happened on the set. I didn't want to talk to anyone because I didn't know who I could trust. But Adrienne and Nadine thought it was hilarious, and as I was certain their plan was doomed to fail, I went along with it.

Thursday I had more scenes with Hunter. Just the two of us (and the entire production crew, and some extra security, but still) in the set of his house. During the scenes Lady Elizabeth was supposed to get Hayden to fall in love with her by being all fake sweet and fake vulnerable, and telling him that Sabrina had done horrible things to her – which wasn't true. At the very end of the scene Hayden had to lean in very close to Lady Elizabeth and almost kiss her, changing his mind at the last minute because he is an honourable boy who doesn't kiss other girls behind his girlfriend's back, even if it does look as if his girlfriend has suddenly become evil.

"Cut!" Suzie shouted to my mixed relief and disappointment as Hunter's lips were millimetres away from mine. As usual, I blushed. I didn't know what it was about Hunter that made me blush; he was nothing like

Danny – they were as different as day and night. Hunter wasn't my type at all, not even back in the day when I was in love with Justin De Souza and had a thing for blond-haired, blue-eyed boys with dreamy smiles. And most importantly, he was the toughest girl in school's boyfriend, a girl who I called my friend even if she did scare me half the time. And we all know that no true friend ever goes after her friend's boyfriend; it just isn't done.

Still, every time Hunter was near me, whether as himself or Hayden, it played havoc with my skin tone. Maybe I was allergic to him in the same way I was allergic to horses.

"Ruby!" Suzie told me. "I love that you blushed when he went in to kiss you. That is so sweet. And Hunter, you looked really tempted to kiss Ruby then. Good work!"

Hunter looked at me and shrugged. "That's because I really was tempted to kiss you," he said sort of under his breath as he walked off. I stood stock still for a moment or two and looked around in case anyone, particularly Adrienne, might have heard him. And then I checked the script just in case what he had said was a line. But it wasn't.

Had Hunter just said that he was tempted to kiss me or had I been hallucinating?

The thought of it made my cheeks burn all the more brightly and I stuck my chin inside the neck of my T-shirt as I headed back to the girls' dressing room. Luckily it was empty because Adrienne, Nadine and the others weren't on set. I sat down and looked at myself in the mirror and told myself a few things to help me clear my mind.

1. I don't even really fancy Hunter. He's just so good-looking in such an obvious way that me blushing whenever he is around is a purely physical thing that I myself have nothing to do with. It is my body's work alone – exactly like getting goose bumps or heat rash.

2. Hunter is Adrienne's boyfriend and even if she would drop him in a second to date Sean Rivers, at the moment he belongs to her. It doesn't matter whether or not he thought about kissing me and whether or not I might have kissed him back. Neither or us has a choice in who we kiss if we don't want to be killed by Adrienne.

3. It has only been a few days since Danny and I officially split up. And I don't properly feel like we have split up yet because I haven't seen him when we haven't been going out together, so I don't know how to feel. And anyway, I still miss him.

4. Sean is coming on Friday and he hates me. I don't have time to think about kissing anybody! I have to try

and work out how to make Sean my friend again so that at least something will be OK back at home when – if – I ever get back there.

It was that last point which focused my mind, and it was all I could think about for the rest of Thursday and all of Friday morning at school. I trailed around after Nadine and Adrienne, sat where they told me to sit, nodded and laughed at all of Zach's jokes and avoided looking Hunter in the eye, which as it turned out was easy because he didn't look at me either.

But I did all of that stuff like a robot stuck on autopilot because inside my head my mind was somewhere else completely. It was racing, galloping, hurtling towards the moment when my mum would pick me up from school and drive me to *The Carl Vine Show* studio where Sean would be waiting for me.

When you know something like that is happening, something that you don't want to happen very much because you are scared of it, something strange happens to time. It slows down and speeds up at the same time.

On a normal day you might not think that thirty minutes until home time was very long at all. But on a day when you have to do something you don't want to face, something you're scared of, you count every single precious minute that stands between you and your appointment with fate. You stretch it out and slow it down, hoping that if you can just concentrate hard enough you'll be able to turn back time. Yet despite how scared I was at the thought of seeing Sean and the look on his face when he saw me, I couldn't wait for it to be over too. I was wishing away the very minutes that I wanted to hold on to because ever since I had turned on the report on C! the Celebrity Channel and seen what I had accidentally done to Sean, that had been almost all I could think about. It had been the cause of my break-up with Danny and the fact that my two best friends didn't seem to be speaking to me. It was the reason I'd been stalked by a journalist. Nothing had gone quite right since that moment, not even getting the part on *Hollywood High*.

So I hoped that whether or not I managed to make things OK with Sean again, at least after I had seen him I'd be able to stop worrying about seeing him. It was a small comfort, but it was the only one I had to hold on to.

"So you're going to Wide Open Universe Studios now, aren't you?" Adrienne asked me as we walked out of school. "Can't I come with you?" She had ditched Nadine whom she was supposed to be supporting in her soccer game to try and persuade me to let her tag along.

"No," I said, forcing myself to be firm with her, which she really didn't like. "I'm sorry, you really can't come. It's film stuff. I'm not allowed to take friends."

"Are you meeting Sean?" she asked, looking at me acutely.

"Yes, I am," I said, seeing no point in lying about it.

"I *really* want to meet him," Adrienne said, her tone just on the edge of a threat.

"Well, you will at the premiere, when you're all dressed up and looking even more beautiful than usual."

"I guess," Adrienne said, half pouting, half smiling. "Well, tell him all about me, OK?"

"I will," I assured her because it was pointless saying that Sean wouldn't be interested in her. She'd never believe it.

And then my mum pulled up at the curb and I realised that all those minutes between me seeing Sean were almost up.

This was it.

THE CARL VINE SHOW
EXCLUSIVE INTERVIEW WITH SEAN RIVERS AND RUBY PARKER
APPROVED INTERVIEW QUESTIONS

FOR SEAN RIVERS

1. TELL ME ABOUT YOUR NEW FILM, *THE LOST TREASURE OF KING ARTHUR.*

2. IS IT A FILM YOU ENJOYED MAKING?

3. WHAT CAN YOU SAY ABOUT THE RUMORS THAT ART DUBROVNIK BULLIED YOU ON THE FILM SET FORCING YOU TO WORK WHEN YOU WEREN'T PHSYICALLY OR MENTALLY ABLE?

4. WHILE YOU WERE SHOOTING THE FILM YOU AND YOUR CO-STAR RUBY PARKER PARTIED HARD SO HARD YOU ALMOST GOT ARRESTED FOR DIAMOND THEFT. CAN YOU TELL US WHY THAT HAPPENED?

5. IS IT TRUE THAT YOUR MOTHER FORCED YOU TO LEAVE ACTING AGAINST YOUR WILL?

6. TELL ME THE REAL REASON YOU DECIDED TO LEAVE ACTING AND RETIRE FROM THE PUBLIC EYE.

7. HOW DO YOU FEEL NOW THAT YOUR PRIVACY HAS BEEN SO CRUELLY INVADED?

8. WHO DO YOU BLAME?

<u>FOR RUBY PARKER</u>

1. THIS IS YOUR FIRST MAJOR FILM ROLE – HOW DOES IT FEEL FOR YOU TO BE IN THE FULL GLARE OF THE MEDIA AT SUCH A YOUNG AGE?

2. DO YOU REGRET GIVING AWAY INFORMATION THAT LED TO THE INVASION OF SEAN'S PRIVACY?

Chapter Fourteen

Suddenly, there Sean was, standing right in front of me.

It wasn't just him and me though. It was his mum, my mum, Lisa Wells, a whole load of people from Wide Open Universe and some Carl Vine production people, all standing around in the celebrities' reception talking at once. Except for me and Sean that is. We didn't say anything. We just looked at each other from opposite sides of the room.

Sean's face was perfectly still, no hint of his trademark smile. But I didn't think I could see any flash of anger or hatred either. He did look tired though, and no wonder because he had only got off a plane an hour or so earlier.

"So," the producer said, "let's get you two into make-up. Follow me, guys, and I'll show you your dressing room." As Sean and I did as we were told, I realised that the whole entourage of parents, publicists and goodness knows who else was coming too.

"Hold on," Sean said, raising his hand as he noticed the same thing. Everybody fell silent. "We don't need all of you in make-up, do we? If you don't mind, I'd like a few minutes to talk to Ruby on my own anyway. We have a few things we need to discuss."

Sean walked off alone towards the dressing room and, full of trepidation, I followed him.

Once we were alone I made myself look at him.

"Look, Sean," I spoke before he could, "I know you hate me, but please believe me when I say that I am *so* sorry. I really, really am – it was a silly mistake. I had no idea—"

"I don't hate you, Ruby, you idiot," Sean said, and for the first time I saw the hint of a smile around his mouth.

"You don't?" I asked him, amazed. "Are you sure?"

"Yes, I'm sure." Sean chuckled briefly before his face grew serious again. "When it first happened, when I got up that morning, pulled back my drapes and was nearly blinded by the camera flashes – the photographers had climbed up *ladders* – *then* I hated you. Until that moment I was really happy. I liked being anonymous, living it that little house with Mom. Going to school with almost regular kids. Being an almost regular kid myself. And when I realised that it had been blown wide open by *you*? Well, I was angry. But I didn't hate you for long." This time Sean's smile was sad. "I wish you hadn't said anything, Ruby, but I know you didn't do it to hurt me. Of course I don't hate you."

"But I broke a promise," I protested as if I wanted him to be angry with me, which I suppose partly I did. "I promised that I wouldn't talk about you to anyone, and I did, on national TV, in front of twenty million viewers!"

Amazingly Sean laughed. "I know – that was a pretty radical way to break a promise!"

"I don't understand," I said. "Sean, don't be nice to me just because you are a nice person. Shout at me, call me names if you want. I'm ready for it. I *deserve* it."

Sean shook his head and sat down heavily in one of the black swivel chairs. He revolved slowly for one complete circle.

"No, you don't deserve that," he said. "Nobody deserves that. Anyway, like Danny said, it wasn't really your fault. There are a whole lot of other people that want a piece of me that come first on the blame list. My dad for stirring things up with Art and trying to ruin my life with Mom, Carl Vine for asking you those questions, and the whole of the press who think it's OK to go and camp outside the house of a fifteen-year-old kid and bully a thirteen-year-old on the set of her show. Those are the people I blame, not you."

"Oh, you heard about that," I said. "I didn't say anything!"

"I know you didn't. It must have been horrible."

"It feels wrong that you're being so nice to me," I said. "Like I've got off too easily."

Sean shrugged. "Don't worry. When you get back, Annie still wants to scratch your eyes out."

"And Nydia?"

"Nydia is worried about you, Ruby. She gave me a letter to give you. Their PC has broken and her mum confiscated her phone because she ran up a massive bill calling this boy she met at the auditions of *Totally Busted*. He lives in – wait for it – Glasgow!"

"Nydia's met a boy! Cool!" I exclaimed, then I realised what he'd said. "You mean Nydia doesn't hate me either? She's still my friend?"

"I don't think you've fallen out with either of them really," Sean said. "Annie is angry on my behalf and said a few typical Anne-Marie style things in the heat of the moment, but she didn't mean them. And Nydia is just worried that the longer you're here, the less likely you'll be the same old Ruby when you get back."

"I've only been here five minutes," I said sadly, sitting down next to him. "How can I have changed that much?" We both made one slow revolution in our chairs.

"The thing is, Rubes," Sean said, "this town can change you completely before you've had time to even take a breath. Trust me, I know."

"That is true, I suppose," I said. "Have you *seen* my mother?"

Sean laughed and nodded. "Your mum does look different," he said. "But then again – have you seen *you*?"

"*Me?*" I laughed. "I don't look different."

"Ruby," Sean said. "Look in the mirror."

Confused, I turned my chair to face my reflection in the big make-up mirror and looked at myself with fresh eyes. And to my surprise, Sean was right. In the few short weeks I had been here, the old Ruby, with her scruffy hair and misbuttoned cardigan, had vanished. The girl looking back at me now had her hair styled to perfection and natural-look eye make-up and a touch of lip gloss expertly applied. Ruby, the girl who refused to be ruled by fashion, was dressed in a mint-green twinset and white denim miniskirt with white low-heeled pumps. I looked like every other Beaumont girl. No, that wasn't true. I didn't look like Tina, who had her own personal style. I looked like a clone of Adrienne, only much less beautiful and, more importantly, much less comfortable than she did.

I didn't look like me at all any more.

"Oh," I said, my eyes widening.

"I'm not saying you don't look good," Sean said. "You actually look pretty cute. But you definitely look different."

I turned to him. "But I am me, Sean," I told him. "I look like this because this is how people look out here – you know that better than anyone. Look at you in your electric-blue suit and white T-shirt. You haven't worn that because that's 'naturally you', have you? But it doesn't matter about the costume as long as you're true to yourself on the inside."

Sean nodded slowly. "You're right, Ruby," he said. "You're absolutely right. I'm just worried about you, that's why I'm saying this stuff. I don't want the same thing that happened to me to happen to you. But as long as you're still sweet, slightly mental, totally cool Ruby on the inside – you're right, it doesn't matter that you look like brunette Barbie."

I thought about "Tragic Tina", a perfectly nice and probably very interesting girl that I had been mean to for no good reason except that it made my life easier with Adrienne. And I thought about how I'd been doing everything that Adrienne and Nadine told me to do because I was too scared to stand up to them and be myself. That wasn't like me at all. Perhaps I *had* changed on the inside. I thought I was just going along with Adrienne for a quiet life, but maybe I was starting to become like her too.

"I want to go home," I said out of the blue. "I don't like it here, Sean. Mum's gone all power-crazed and there are these two girls in *Hollywood High* who I'm letting turn me into a personality zombie, and I haven't spoken to Dad in ages."

"Then go home," Sean said, as if it were that simple.

"I can't," I said. "I can't just go home."

"Why not?"

I had to think for a second. "Because I have four more weeks of shooting to do for *Hollywood High*, and there is no way my mum will let me drop out of that even if I could, which I don't think I can because of contracts and stuff. And anyway, I think she likes it here with Jeremy. She keeps looking for 'my next project'. I'm sure she wants us to live here."

"But if you're unhappy…" Sean said.

"I can't," I said. "Not yet. But when I've finished *Hollywood High* I'm going to tell Mum I want to go home."

"OK," Sean said. "I have just one other thing to say, Ruby, that I want you to remember."

"What's that?" I asked him.

"In Hollywood one minute they love you and the next

minute they hate you. And you never know when everything is going to change. So just be ready and remember you can't take it personally, because whatever they say about you, none of them really know you. And anyway you have four friends at home who care about you, even if one of them thinks she isn't talking to you at the moment."

"Three friends," I reminded him. "Danny chucked me."

"I know, but Danny still thinks of you as a friend," Sean said.

"Really?" I asked him, brightening a little. "Do you think he regrets finishing with me?"

Sean looked down at his feet. "Look, Ruby, Danny didn't want me to tell you in case it upset you – but I think you should know. He's dating someone else. This new girl on *Kensington Heights*. Her name is Melody something."

"Oh," I said, stunned. It took a few seconds for the words to sink in and then I realised what they meant. That was the something that Danny had been trying to tell me on his webcam. "You mean he didn't chuck me because of what happened with you?"

"No, Ruby. He just met this other girl and he liked her. When he told me I was more surprised than anyone. I mean, Danny was so into you, but this Melody, she is *really* into Danny. I think she was out to get him from the minute they met."

"Melody," I said. "After all the things he said to me I just thought… Look, I know we're only thirteen, but I just thought we'd survive me being away on holiday!"

"Well, yeah," Sean said, looking a little uncomfortable. "She's a nice girl, but Danny's been different since Melody came along. And since the number one record. If it helps, Annie doesn't like her and Nydia barely speaks to her. And no way is she as cute as you."

"Well, OK, that's OK," I said, finally feeling reality kick in. "That's good actually. I think that's really good because now at least I know it isn't anything I've done. He's gone off me." My voice cracked a little at this point.

"Ruby," Sean said, "he's an idiot. You're a great chick."

"It doesn't matter, not really," I said, shaking my head to stop the threat of tears. "We're just a couple of kids. We're not Romeo and Juliet, after all."

"Thank you, Sean," Carl Vine said, shaking Sean's hand after we had finished the interview. "I really respect you coming over here and addressing these questions. I know it took a lot of guts. I think the public will feel that they now know the truth and will let you get back to the life you want. Who knows, maybe the paps will even let you alone."

"Thanks, Carl," Sean said, switching on his light bulb smile. "And maybe next time you are interviewing an inexperienced thirteen-year-old making her live TV debut on your show, you won't ask her questions you have no business to."

"Ouch," Carl nodded. "I deserved that, kid."

"So," I said to Sean after Carl had gone to talk to some of the production staff, "one last thing to do and then you get your life back."

"Yep," Sean said. "You and me, Ruby, walking that red carpet again!"

"It feels like a lot has changed," I said sadly, "since we walked down the red carpet the first time.

"Well, a lot of things have changed," Sean said. "Changing your life is easy in this business. It's keeping things the same that's impossible."

Later that night I stayed up with Mum and Jeremy, David on my lap, as *The Carl Vine Show* aired our interview. I say "our interview", but all I did was back Sean up and answer my two questions. It was really all about him and I for one was glad about that. He handled it brilliantly, and no matter how much he might hate it, Sean was the definition of a natural in front of the camera.

"He is an amazing boy," Jeremy said as he watched Sean talk about what life with his father had been like, the endless months of work, the cruelty, the punishments. And how Art Dubrovnik and Imogene Grant – not forgetting his good friend Ruby Parker – had helped reunite him with his mom and escape to a new life.

"And so talented," Jeremy added. "It will be a great tragedy if he never returns to acting."

"But he is still acting," I said. "He acts every day at the Academy. Only now he's doing it just for himself and he's happy."

"What's the point of that?" Mum said. Jeremy and I looked at her. "I *mean*," she added quickly, "what's the point of having all that talent and hiding it away? Obviously, there's a lot of point to being happy."

"Good, I'm glad you think so," Jeremy said with a dry smile, winking at me. "He is only a boy after all."

"Well, girls are tougher than boys," Mum said. "Isn't that right, Ruby?"

"Sometimes," I replied. "And sometimes they aren't."

"Anyway," Mum put an arm around me and hugged me to her, "I thought you did really well and the best thing is that now no one can blame you for anything. All we have to do now is keep our fingers crossed and hope that the reviews after the premiere of *King Arthur* won't keep the public away."

"Even if they do," I said, lifting my chin, "I know it's a good film and I'm proud of it."

"And so you should be, Ruby," Jeremy said, smiling at me.

"Then go and be proud in bed," Mum said. "You need your beauty sleep. It's a lunchtime premiere so that means up at six for a shower. Julian, Cary and Simone will be here by seven to start getting us ready."

"Five hours to get ready!" I exclaimed. "Who needs *five hours* to get ready?"

"Film stars do, darling," Mum told me. "So get used to it."

Chapter Fifteen

"Are you OK?" Sean asked me as our stretch limo waited in a queue of identical cars, inching ever closer to the start of the red carpet where Sean and I would get out. I pushed my face against the window so that I could catch a glimpse of Imogene being accompanied by Jeremy. She was wearing a stunning sky-blue gown encrusted with crystals, so she glittered like a summer's day.

"I'm fine," I said, sitting back up and leaving half my make-up imprinted on the glass. Julian, who it seemed was determined to follow me everywhere, tutted and whipped out his kit to swiftly retouch my face.

"I'm sorry if that stuff I told you about Danny upset you," Sean said. "You know that was the last thing I wanted to do."

"You didn't upset me," I replied. "Well, what you told me did a bit, but I'm not staying upset. In fact, if anything, I'm cross with Danny. He was too much of a coward to tell me he'd started going out with someone else and that's not fair. So I'm angry with him and it beats being miserable."

"Good, I *think*," Sean said cautiously. "Look, when you get back things will work themselves out, you'll see."

"Whatever," I said, exactly like Adrienne would. "Oh, that reminds me, you're going to meet two of my new friends today. I'm sorry."

"Sorry? Why?" Sean looked confused.

"You'll see," I said.

At last our car reached the red carpet. I rolled down the window and listened to the crowd cheer. I felt the nerves bubble in my tummy and when I tried to swallow my mouth was dry. But I couldn't get them to turn the limo around and take me home. There was nothing for it but to get out.

Suddenly, my door was opened and the clatter of camera shutters going off nearly deafened me as I did my best to step out of the car in a ladylike fashion. Julian had chosen a lovely pink dress for me, which looked, he said, like an English rose blooming. It had a deep pink satin bodice with a light and whirly chiffon skirt that wafted about in the slight breeze. It was exactly the sort of fairy princess-style dress that I would have adored when I was about five. At the age of thirteen, I still loved it, and more than that I loved the silver high heels that Julian had let me wear, with strict instructions not to fall flat on my face.

And in that second, as the flashlights exploded and the crowd cheered, I really did feel like a film star, and it was the most wonderful and exciting feeling in the world.

Then I realised that everyone was cheering for Sean, which put my feet right back on the earth (or about two inches off it if you counted the heels).

"My lady," Sean said, offering me his arm. "May I escort you?"

I smiled at him. "Don't mind if you do, kind sir," I said in my best Lady Elizabeth voice.

It took us an age to get past all of Sean's fans, who were clamouring for him to sign autographs, have their photo taken with him or begging him to speak to their granny on a mobile phone. Some of them were even so overcome that this might be the last time they got to see him that they were crying their eyes out.

It was incredible to watch Sean working and, amazingly, while he was swamped with requests from fans, a few people even called me over to sign autographs too.

"Sign it to Tina please," a familiar voice said, and when I looked up I realised it was Tina from school.

"Hello!" I said, pleased to see a familiar face in all the madness. "You must have been here since dawn to get right to the front."

"Since 6 a.m," she said, flushing. "Look, I admit it. I think Sean Rivers is a fantastic actor."

"Even though he's only ever done film and no theatre?" I teased her.

Tina laughed. "Well, he's given up film so maybe theatre will be his next choice."

"I think there's a school play next term," I said, laughing too. I called Sean over after he'd stopped being hugged by an old lady.

"This is my friend from school, Tina," I said. "Will you sign her photo of you?"

"Is this the friend you were talking about?" Sean asked me as he signed Tina's autograph.

"Oh no, you don't have to be scared of Tina. It's Adrienne who will terrify you. She terrifies me!"

"Ruby!" Tina looked amazed. "I thought you loved her!"

"Scared stiff of her more like," I said.

"Take care, Tina," Sean said with a smile as he handed her back the photo. "It's cool to meet you." And for a second I was certain that the cool and collected girl

I was used to from school was about to melt into a puddle on the red carpet.

"We'd better go," Sean said. "There's still another mile or so of carpet to go!"

"Bye, Tina," I said, smiling and waving.

"Good luck with Adrienne," Tina called back. "You'll need it!"

It took us half an hour to reach the official photographers where we stood side by side smiling until our faces ached. There were no ill-advised kisses this time. It was funny, I thought, Sean's brief kiss on my lips the last time we had walked the red carpet together had ended up plastered all over the newspapers and nearly cost me my boyfriend. Now I had no boyfriend and there was no way Sean would kiss me, even on the cheek, because he knew that Anne-Marie would kill him if he did.

Finally, we made it into the foyer of the cinema and straightaway I was pounced on by Adrienne and Nadine. Adrienne was dressed in a red number trimmed with matching feathers and Nadine was wearing a white dress that showed off her back.

"Hi!" Adrienne said, literally shoving me out of the way to get to Sean. I tottered on my silver heels and was only saved from falling by a steadying hand from Hunter. Of course I immediately blushed.

"I'm Adrienne Charles, star of new TV hit *Hollywood High*. I'm a huge fan of your work and although I respect your decision to retire from the limelight, I will truly miss your presence on our screens."

"Oh, well," Sean said with a shrug. "There's always DVD rental."

"Hahahahahahhahah!" Adrienne's shriek of laughter made several heads turn.

"Hey, Rubes," Hunter said, smiling at me. "You look great."

"And what about me?" Adrienne asked almost automatically.

"I told you, you look beautiful," Hunter said, rolling his eyes at Sean. "Hey, man," he held out his hand. "I'm Hunter Blake. Cool to meet you."

"And you, dude," Sean said.

Their boys' conversation complete, the *Hollywood High* cast was rounded up by Suzie Blenheim to take their seats inside, but not before she came over and kissed me on the cheek and wished me luck.

I felt Adrienne's eyes on me as Imogene rushed over and gave me and Sean one of her trademark hugs. This event would either make me even more cool or incredibly unpopular with her, I wasn't sure yet. I thought that after the film I'd better do my best to introduce her to everyone famous that I knew (and some that I didn't) so that I could make sure that I stayed on her good side.

And then I realised that that was a stupid thought to have. It was, despite my tendency to do many stupid things, not a *Ruby* thing to do at all.

Sean was right; it was easy to let Hollywood change you for the worse. From now on I was going to get my old self, my Ruby Parker self, back and I wasn't going to let her go again.

Just before we went into the cinema I had an idea. I pulled Lisa over to one side and whispered to her.

She took a step back and smiled at me. "Sure, Ruby," she said. "That's a lovely thought and it will make great press. I'll sort that out for you right away."

"Thank you," I said, and then I was the last cast member to be ushered into the cinema.

The opening credits began to roll.

"You were wonderful," Adrienne told Sean at the after party.

And I would have agreed with her if it hadn't been for the fact that she had her back to me and was trying her best to get Sean alone. Still waiting for the other party guests to arrive, I shrugged and looked around me.

For the party, Wide Open Universe had dressed a sound stage to look like the vaults of the British Museum. There were Zombie Mummy Witches serving drinks and the Lost Knights of the Round Table passing out canapés. Dry ice wafted out from crevices in the floor and millions of fairy lights twinkled above our heads. It was pretty impressive.

Quite a few photographers wandered in and out of the guests, taking shots, and every time one went past Adrienne she automatically posed. It was impressive really, like a kind of celebrity ninja skill.

"She won't stop flirting with Sean until she gets her way," Nadine said in my ear. "She practically trampled me in her rush to get in your car on the way to the party."

I turned around and stared at her in surprise.

"She'd drop Hunter like a stone if she thought Sean Rivers would date her," Nadine continued in a low voice edged with anger. "She doesn't care about the boy she dates; all she cares about is how much publicity he will get her. Pretty scary, huh?"

I hesitated before responding. Nadine had never, ever said anything like that about Adrienne before and I assumed it was because they were so close. In fact, I had to admit that I sort of thought of them as the same person. Like one of those Hollywood couples whose names get melded into one by the press. "Adine" maybe or "Nadrienne". I didn't want to drop myself in it by saying something I shouldn't to Adrienne's best friend. Maybe she was testing me to see how loyal I was and would immediately report back.

"Oh, well, you know Adrienne," I said lightly. "She's naturally friendly, isn't she?"

"Naturally pushy, you mean," Nadine said. "Sean's your friend, you haven't seen him in ages and she's hogged him since the minute she met him. And all because of what she thinks he can do for her career." She sighed. "Honestly, Ruby, I know I have to be friends with the girl, but that doesn't mean I have to like her."

"Actually," I said, "I sort of thought that it did. Adrienne is your best friend."

"My best friend on the *show*," Nadine said, emphasising the last word. "In real life I'd never choose her for a friend at all if I didn't have to."

"But... why do you have to?" I asked her, confused.

Nadine looked at me as if I were an idiot. "The same reason you have to," she told me. "Because if Adrienne likes you, your life is a lot easier. I see her every day, I work with her most days. If I didn't get on with her, my life would be a living hell. It pretty much is anyway, but if she hated me it would be a million times worse. And I'm always on edge, because I may be her best friend now, but she could turn on me tomorrow. I've seen it happen. Look at Tina. The minute she started to have opinions that were different from Adrienne's, Adrienne turned on her."

"Tina and Adrienne used to be friends?"

"*Best* friends," Nadine told me. "And then along came *Hollywood High* and I got cast as her best friend on the show, and before I knew it she was telling everybody we were best friends in real life too. She'd never spoken two words to me before that. Said I was a sports freak and a waste of space."

I looked over at Adrienne who was tossing her hair in Hunter's face as she talked to Sean. Sean caught my eye and I guessed that the panicked look in his eyes was a plea for me to go and rescue him.

"I can't believe you've never told me this before," I told Nadine.

"She never leaves us alone, and besides I didn't mean to tell you today," Nadine said. "It's just that sometimes she gets too much. Please don't tell her what I've said, will you?" I shook my head.

"I won't, but, well – surely it would be better if you were just honest with her?"

"You don't know what it's like for Adrienne to hate you," Nadine told me.

"It can't be that bad," I said.

Nadine looked levelly at me. "Oh no? Ask Tina what it's like."

Sean was now frantically making faces at me every time Adrienne glanced away from him. "Come on," I said to Nadine. "Sean needs rescuing."

But I thought about what Nadine had said about Tina, and I realised that Nadine was right. It took a really strong, brave girl to choose to be on the wrong side of Adrienne.

"Oh, Ruby, you again," Adrienne said with an icy smile as Nadine and I joined her, Hunter and Sean."

"I was just telling Adrienne all about Anne-Marie," Sean said. "And her new modelling contract for H&M."

"Oh, yes," I said. "Sean's girlfriend really is beautiful. And she does kick-boxing too."

"You obviously have excellent taste in girls," Adrienne said, fluttering her lashes at Sean, who was now looking positively frightened.

"Not really," he said. "Just the girls next door, which is the only kind of girl I meet now that I'm a show-business nobody."

"I can't believe that you're really going to give up the

limelight," Adrienne purred. "I saw you out there with the crowd. You loved it!"

"I was just doing my job," Sean replied with a shrug. "Well, what *was* my job, I'm retiring as soon as this party is over."

"Wow, this is *so* cool! Like a huge theatre set!" I heard a familiar voice at my side and turned round to find Tina.

"Here she is," Lisa said. She smiled at the other two girls whose jaws had dropped right down to their peep-toed sandals. "We took her out of the crowd and Julian even found her a frock to wear. Really nice idea, Ruby."

"Hi, Tina," I said brightly, remembering my pact to myself to be myself. "I *thought* you'd like to come to the party."

"Ruby, thanks so much for getting me invited!" Tina said happily. Julian had put her in a peacock-green and blue dress that made her look great.

"You invited *her*?" Adrienne asked me incredulously, her nasty tone making her look ugly. "Is this some kind of joke, Ruby? Because it isn't funny."

"I saw Tina in the crowd," I said. "I thought it would be nice to invite a fellow Beaumont girl."

"She should have stayed there," Adrienne retorted. "She belongs in a crowd where you don't have to look at her."

"Hey," Sean said. "You can't speak to people like that!"

Adrienne realised that she'd shown her worst side in front of the boy she was trying her hardest to impress. "Sean, this is not the kind of person people like us hang out with!"

"If Ruby likes Tina then I do." Sean turned to us. "Come on, guys, let's go and talk to Imogene. She'd love to meet you, Tina."

Sean put his arm through a stunned Tina's and began to lead her away. I hesitated, not sure of what to do next. Adrienne was fuming.

"You made a fool of me in front of Sean Rivers," she hissed.

"I didn't," I said reasonably. "You did that yourself."

"Are you calling me stupid?" Adrienne replied. I glanced at Nadine hoping for some support, but she didn't say anything.

"I'm just saying, why don't you come over and meet Imogene Grant and hang out with me and Tina for a bit. You were friends once."

"How did you know that?" Adrienne asked me sharply.

"Tina told me," I lied, glancing quickly at Nadine.

"Look, Ruby, you can't just swan into my school and tell me how to behave and who to hang out with. I've made you into someone halfway decent that cool kids consider hanging out with. Without me you're nothing."

"Actually," I said steadily, "I think that without you I'm a nicer person. So I don't care if you don't like me any more, Adrienne, because I don't like you. You're not a very nice person."

"Whatever. We're leaving, right, Nadine?" she told her friend furiously.

Nadine looked at me and then at Adrienne. "Yes," she said dully. "We're leaving."

I caught Nadine's arm as Adrienne marched off without even a second glance at Hunter.

"Why don't you come with me and Tina?" I whispered.

Nadine shook her head. "You're leaving in a few weeks, Ruby, so maybe you can take the pain she's going to give you from now until then. But I can't. And listen, when I don't talk to you on Monday, don't take it personally. I actually really like you."

As Nadine left I saw Hunter watching me thoughtfully. "You're pretty brave," he told me. "She's going to be out to get you now."

I shrugged. "All I did was ask Tina to the party."

"I'm glad you did. She's a cool chick," Hunter said.

"Really?" I replied. "But you never talk to her usually."

"I like the theatre stuff she does. Her last play was

really good. I'd join if... well, you know why I can't."

I shook my head. "I don't, Hunter. First Nadine and now you. Adrienne is just a girl. A pretty scary one I'll give you that, but only because we all let her be. We give her power." I laughed, feeling suddenly free. "I mean, you're her *boyfriend*! Don't tell me you're only dating her because you are frightened not to!"

"I'm not actually really dating her at all," Hunter said. "We've never actually gone out on a date. She finds me completely boring, and I'd rather kiss a frog. Have you ever seen us hold hands? When I got the part in *Hollywood High* Adrienne thought if we said we were dating in real life it would be good for our profiles, and she was right. We got a lot of press. I kept going along with it because I hadn't met a girl I really wanted to date... until now."

"Right!" I said, getting on my high horse. "In that case you should tell Adrienne that your fake relationship is off and ask out the girl you really like right away."

"You think so?" Hunter asked me, a slow smile spreading over his face.

"I do," I said firmly.

"OK," he said. "Ruby?"

"Yes?" I replied, suddenly feeling my cheeks ignite.

"Would you go to the Valentine's dance with me?"

Hi Rubes!!!!!

I am sorry that I haven't sent you any e-mails recently and if you've sent me some I'm sorry that I haven't replied either. Our computer broke and Mum has grounded me totally except for school and work so I couldn't get to a cyber café. It's a long story. I'll tell you all about it when you get back.

Hope you are OK about Danny. Me and Anne-Marie were so surprised. One minute he was, "Oh, I miss Ruby" and the next he brought this girl Melody to the café for hot chocolate. He's just not like Danny any more, it's weird. She is boring Ruby. Anne-Marie says if she is a Melody then she must be a lullaby because every time she sees her she wants to fall asleep!

They have started to show
the trailers for your film
at the cinema and on
telly. It's very exciting!
No reviews here yet. I
hope you don't think I was
in a mood with you because of the
Sean thing. I wasn't ever because I
know you. You are sometimes a
thicko, but mainly you are the
best person I know, and the best
friend anyone could have.

Ooooh I have so much to tell
you and you are not here!
Hopefully Mum and Dad will
get to Currys and buy us a
new PC soon. I don't think
I'll ever be allowed a mobile
phone again (same long
story). Come back sooon!
I miss you
Nyds

XXXXXXXXXXXX ❤❤❤❤❤❤❤❤

Chapter Sixteen

I read Nydia's letter for about the hundredth time because whenever things got really terrible it cheered me up for a few minutes. Although you might think that being asked to the Valentine's dance by the best-looking boy in school might be the furthest thing from terrible that anything could be, you'd be wrong.

Well not wrong about Hunter asking. That was nice, *if* confusing. It's just that from the moment he did it, everything I had just about managed to hold together until then started to disintegrate in front of my eyes, along with my life. Or at least what I thought was my life. That of an actress, a celebrity, maybe even a film star.

At first I just sort of stood there and stared at Hunter, looking probably quite a lot like a very surprised bunny rabbit about to be flattened by a large truck. I should have learnt by now that boys generally appreciate a direct answer and preferably within two or three minutes of asking. Standing and staring never usually gets you anywhere. It also gives them far too much time to reconsider.

After a while Hunter laughed which unnerved me even more than him asking me to the dance.

"Ruby, you sure know how to make a guy squirm," he said with a rueful smile that made my face turn a lovely shade of beetroot.

"But you're going with Adrienne," I said. He shook his head.

"Not any more. Look, on Monday you're going to be at the top of her most hated list. I thought you could do with some company there."

"I feel like I've started a war. All I did was invite Tina to the party and not let Adrienne get off with my friend's boyfriend."

"That *is* starting a war in Adrienne's eyes," Hunter told me. "You've threatened her position of power. She doesn't like that. She'll want it back. You're her rival now. I think you'll need all the friends you can get."

"And you'd go to the dance with me knowing she'll do the same to you?"

"I like you, Ruby," Hunter said, taking a step closer to me. "So – what do you say? Will you go to the dance with me or not?"

I took a step backwards and nearly fell off my heels.

"I don't know, Hunter," I stuttered. "I've only just split up with my boyfriend. I might be on the rebound. I don't know if I'm on the rebound because he was my first boyfriend and I don't know what it's like to be on the rebound. I just know that you're not supposed to go out with people when you are on it because it always ends in disaster."

"It's just a dance, Ruby," Hunter chuckled. "You're going back to the UK in a couple of weeks. I'm not asking you to marry me!"

"Oh, right," I said, feeling a little bit deflated. "Well, OK then. Yes, I will go to the dance with you if you're sure it's just as friends."

"Well, I didn't say *that*," Hunter said before disappearing into the crowd.

Of course he knew how to make an exit. He was a drama-school kid.

I worried about going to the dance with Hunter for the rest of that day and all night, about whether or not it was a good idea for him to make Adrienne his enemy, about what he meant by asking me to go with him. If he really was being just a pal or if at some point in the evening he might want to kiss me. I thought it might be nice to kiss Hunter, even on the rebound, but I was still worried about it. I have only ever kissed three boys. Justin de Souza and that was a screen kiss, Sean Rivers and that was by mistake and over in three seconds, and Danny. What if Hunter tried to kiss me and I was rubbish, or cried or something because of Danny?

That was what I worried about the night after the party when everybody else was celebrating and congratulating each other.

But I shouldn't have bothered worrying about any of it because I was about to find out that I had a lot worse things to worry about.

The press reviews came on Sunday morning. The papers and magazines were delivered to Jeremy's house at the same time as Sean was flying back to normality and home.

Normally, there are several previews of a film before it is released to the general public so that reviews and critics can write about it and so give it more publicity. But sometimes, when they think that the film is bad, or if as with *The Lost Treasure of King Arthur*, there has been negative publicity surrounding it, they don't screen previews because they don't want anything bad written about it before it is released.

Maybe the waiting made the film critics angry, or maybe they just had it in for Art, like Jeremy said when we first came out to Hollywood. Maybe they really did hate my film because not one review was good. Not good about the film, not good about Imogene, not good about Jeremy or even Sean and, especially, *especially* not good about me.

As I read them I began to feel exactly like that time when I was in the cubicle in the girls' loos and heard Menakshi Shah and Jade Caruso talking about me, only a million times worse. What Menakshi and Jade had said was old news. What the American critics thought about me and my acting was all horribly, painfully new.

At first as I scanned the page all I felt was anger on behalf of Art and everyone else. They weren't writing about the film we made. And it was not the film that I had heard an audience clap and cheer with a standing ovation at the premiere.

And then I saw my name on the page and it was like having the worst kind of nightmare and realising that you are awake. I forced myself to read on.

Newcomer British actress Ruby Parker showed early promise, one paper wrote. *But it was a promise that soon faded as she turned in a wooden and lacklustre performance, making me feel I'd eaten a very heavy visual meal that had given me indigestion of the eyes. It is inconceivable why Dubrovnik chose to cast this drama-school amateur when he could have had his pick of a host of talented professionals.*

I didn't realise I was biting my lip until I tasted blood on my tongue. This wasn't just critical, it was vicious.

"'Over the hill and overdramatic', he called me," Jeremy said, gently taking the paper from my hands. "I know it hurts, Ruby, especially when you've given something your all, but I promise you it's just one person's opinion. The critics say what they like, not what's true. Especially rags like these."

"He's right, Rube," Mum said, putting her hands on my shoulder, but I shrugged her off and picked up another paper, searching for my name before reading out loud.

"'Young Miss Parker obviously tried her best as Polly Harris, but her best was very far from what was required to save the film from the doldrums. The role was too big for her to handle and she failed to light up the screen with even a spark of charm or any acting ability. She would have done better to audition for the lead in the school play. Or perhaps she did and they turned her down.'"

"Well that's simply not true!" my mum exclaimed. "Please, Ruby, don't upset yourself. This is just a blip."

"It is true," I replied faintly, not really hearing her.

"I've never been given the lead in a school play."

I snatched up another review, in a magazine this time. Mum stood looking at Jeremy wringing her hands together.

"'Ruby Parker might be a big deal on Brit TV, but it looks like she'll be small potatoes on the silver screen over here. She did nothing to improve the turkey that not even Art Dubrovnik could save. My sources tell me we're soon to see her in hit show *Hollywood High*. Let's hope she doesn't sink that like she did *The Lost Treasure of King Arthur*. Lost treasure? If you ask me it should have stayed lost.'"

I went to pick up another paper, but Mum took it away.

"Ruby, listen to me," she said firmly. "You know about this. They prepare you for this at school and you know that if you want to be an actress you have to be tough, thick-skinned. Part of what you do is allowing people to judge you. When you make a film or a TV show that part of you is public property. People feel they have the right to say what they like about you. It doesn't mean it's true. It doesn't mean it's right. You have to remember that and get on with things just as before."

"Your mum is right, Ruby," Jeremy said carefully. "Gosh, I've had some terrible reviews in my time, much worse than these. But it wouldn't surprise me if in a few years time these same critics will be praising you in the very work they slated."

"Besides," Mum said, smiling encouragingly, "Lisa called early this morning and told us that it looks as if the takings over the first weekend are set to make back production costs already! So it doesn't matter what the papers say, people *are* going to see it."

"They are going to see Sean Rivers' last movie, or because Imogene Grant's in it," I said flatly. "They're not going to see it because I was good."

Even though I had just got up I suddenly felt incredibly tired. "I'm going to my room," I said, picking David up.

"Ruby!" Mum called after me, but I didn't stop. I ran up the stairs, shut the door and sat on the floor, leaning my back against it.

I had never had a review written about me before. When I was Angel on *Kensington Heights* sometimes I might get mentioned in a summary of soap plots in the *Radio Times*, but never in a really cruel way. "Poor old downtrodden Angel," they'd write, "the most unfortunate teen in soap." Never anything horrid about me, Ruby Parker.

I felt like every part of my body was bruised, on the inside as well as the outside.

There hadn't been one good review, not one. And all of those writers couldn't be wrong, even if that's what Mum and Jeremy wanted me to believe. If they all thought I was a terrible, talentless actress then they had to be right. After all, how did I get here? How did I get to Hollywood? Was it really because of any talent? No.

I got the part in *Kensington Heights* without even trying when I was six years old and they only cast me because I was cute, not because I was talented.

I got the part in *The Lost Treasure of King Arthur* because I had been in *Kensington Heights* for so many years. Art Dubrovnik told me that himself when he offered me the part. He said that my experience counted for a lot. I wasn't the best girl he auditioned. I was just the most experienced he could find at short notice.

And I got the part in *Hollywood High* because of a TV interview I was doing for *The Lost Treasure of King Arthur*. OK, I passed the audition, but it wasn't because I was right for the role. It was for the publicity that surrounded me after I let slip Sean's hideaway.

I dragged myself up from the floor and went over to the mirror. As I stared at my reflection I suddenly realised something.

I wasn't *meant* to be in Hollywood at all. I was the *wrong* girl in the *wrong* place at the *wrong* time. I wasn't meant to be a film star or a TV star or any kind of star. I wasn't even meant to be an actress, because I wasn't nearly good enough. I was just a girl who liked acting and who by some terrible, terrible mistake ended up in the limelight where she didn't belong.

I knew exactly what I had to do. I had to put things right straightaway.

I ran back downstairs and found Mum. "I'm ready," I told her urgently.

"Ready for what, darling?" Mum asked me. "Breakfast?"

"Ready to go home," I told her. "Remember? You promised when I said I wanted to go home that you would take me. Well, I want to go home now, Mum."

My mum put down her cup of tea and put her arms around me.

"Listen, Ruby," she said, "this is hard for you, I know. What those people wrote about you was so unfair. But in a few days all those reviews will be in recycling bins and no one will remember them. You'll feel better, I promise."

"Why are you so keen for me to feel better, Mum?" I asked, pushing away from her. "Better over Danny, better about these reviews. Better over you and Dad. Well, maybe I'm not ready to feel better. Maybe I shouldn't feel better because what they wrote about me was true. I've been thinking about it and it suddenly clicked. I can't really act at all."

"Rubbish!" Mum's snap surprised me. She was trying hard not to be angry with me. "Look, Ruby, in another couple of weeks you'll be finished on *Hollywood High*. Then we'll take stock and see what our position is."

"NO!" I half shouted and half sobbed. "NO! Don't you understand? I don't want to go back to Beaumont! I don't want to shoot any more *Hollywood High*, I DON'T WANT TO! I WANT TO GO HOME NOW!"

"WELL, YOU CAN'T!" my mum shouted back, shocking me into silence. "You have a contract, Ruby, a contract that I signed on your behalf, and you will fulfil that contract because that is what you do when you are an actor. You meet your commitments and you don't give up! So what if you've had a few knocks, a couple of bad reviews. Well then, you pick yourself up, dust yourself off and you do the best work you possibly can on *Hollywood High*. And you show everybody, *everybody*, that they are wrong about you." Mum took a breath and attempted a smile. "That is what you are going to do, Ruby. Do you understand?"

"But, Mum," I said, feeling tears thicken my voice. "Mum, I just want to go home."

"Not yet, Ruby," Mum said, kissing the top of my head

and giving me a stiff hug. "Look, I don't mean to upset you. I'm just trying to show that if you want to be in this industry, you have to be as tough as it is. Do you understand?"

I nodded. "I do," I said because she was right.

What I didn't know how to do was tell her that I didn't want to *be* in the industry any more. I didn't want to be in show business. I had no talent. It was official.

But I didn't want to let her down, partly because I wanted her to be proud of me and partly because I was afraid to. So I let her give me breakfast and I plastered a smile back on my face. Just a few more weeks, I told myself. I just have to stick it out for a few more weeks and then it will be over.

And what would happen after that?

I couldn't even think about it.

RUBY PARKER

Chapter Seventeen

When I decided to stick it out, I
hadn't counted on just how bad it
would be at Beaumont.

As Mum dropped me off on Monday, Tina and Hunter
were waiting for me.

"We thought we'd walk you in," Tina said.

"Yeah," Hunter told me. "Tina is introducing me to the
ranks of the disaffected."

"Dissa-what?" I asked him.

"Kids ostracised by Adrienne."

"Ostra-?"

"People she hates," Hunter said, chuckling at me.

"I knew that," I said, feeling myself blush. It was
stupid really. I'd known him now for several weeks.
You'd think my skin would have got immune to him by
now, especially when I had far more important things to
worry about than random blushing. "Does Adrienne
know that she hates you yet?" I asked Hunter.

"Not yet," Hunter told me. "But this should help let
her know." He took my hand in his.

"Hunter, I'm not sure…" I began in somebody else's voice, because mine was not normally that high pitched and girly.

"Relax, Ruby," Hunter told me. "I've been in one fake relationship for a long time. What better way to end it than with another."

"Genius," Tina said with a little hop. "She's going to implode."

"Why is it that people frequently want to pretend to go out with me?" I said, but very quietly under my breath, because after all if Hunter really did want to date me, I think I might run a million miles in the opposite direction in terror. It wasn't like it had been with Danny, when I sort of got to like him without really noticing.

Going out with Danny had been mostly easy. But how do you date a boy you find hard to look in the eye because he's so handsome? Not to mention one who very soon will be on the other side of the Atlantic from you. Although that might make him easier to date because then at least I wouldn't have to look at him.

As we walked around the corner, my hand feeling decidedly odd in Hunter's, we bumped right into Adrienne, Nadine and the rest of the witchy coven.

Nadine's eyes nearly popped out of her head when she saw me holding Hunter's hand. Adrienne's face didn't move a muscle.

"What's going on?" she asked Hunter in clipped tones.

"Look, Adrienne," Hunter said calmly with the hint of a smile, "I'm sorry you have to find out like this – but Ruby and I are dating now."

There was a gasp from the girls behind Adrienne.

"*You* are dating *her*?" Adrienne said with a harsh laugh. "That loser, that – what did the papers call her? Oh yeah, that's right: a wooden and lacklustre failure who wouldn't even get a part in a school play. You'd really give *me* up for that? The girl who describes herself as fun, friendly and fashionable when she really meant to say fat, frumpy and a fraud?"

"Well, I want to give you up. I'm sure of that," Hunter said, igniting another flurry of shocked noise behind Adrienne, although I thought I saw the hint of a smile flash across Nadine's face.

Adrienne narrowed her eyes into tiny slits and walked towards me, stopping so close that her nose was just a hair's breadth away from mine. I was sure I was about to find out what it was like to be punched by another girl.

"You're welcome to him," she hissed in my face. "He's a loser just like you, Ruby. To think I wasted all that time hanging out with you, being bored out of my brain because I thought you'd help my career. I count myself lucky that you haven't dragged me down with you. The day you leave here won't come too soon for me."

She tossed her head as she whipped round so that her hair lashed me in the face. "Come on, girls," she said with a click of her fingers. "Let's go."

Hunter, Tina and I stood there as Adrienne and her pack retreated.

"Today's going to be fun," I said. "I have scenes to shoot with her after school."

"Ruby," Hunter said, "can you let go of my hand now? You're kind of hurting me."

I'm used to my life being a bit like a rollercoaster, up one minute and down the next, but it seemed to me that this particular stretch of rollercoaster was going down, down and down with no prospect of it climbing upwards any time soon.

As sweet as Hunter, Tina and their friends were, they could only protect me so much from Adrienne's wrath and each passing day seemed to get worse.

I'd find blown-up copies of my bad reviews plastered all over the corridors. Photographs of me that had been scanned into someone's PC and changed, blowing me up so I looked like a great big balloon that was about to pop. Even worse, the photo of my mother that had appeared in *People's Choice Magazine* was strewn around the school.

I'd walk past people who only a few days ago were falling over themselves to be nice to me and they'd snigger, muttering insults directed at me. I'd feel their eyes on me and I'd know they were talking about me even if I couldn't hear what they were saying. It was just what Tina must have felt when I did the same to her. I told myself I deserved it.

Then there was the superglue on my seat that ripped a hole in my linen trousers and which Mum had to get off my leg with nail varnish remover. Someone poured shampoo in my school bag, ruining all of the work that was due to be sent back to Miss Greenstreet that week. Chewing gum was stuck in my hair. Tina cut it out with nail scissors in the girls' loo. And I got tripped up in the corridor so that I fell flat on my face.

Mum asked me about the glue and the missing clump of hair from the back of my head. But I just made up a Ruby-like excuse that she seemed to accept. And when she told me off for ruining my homework with shampoo, I just shrugged.

It's funny because when I played Angel on *Kensington Heights*, girls used to write to me all the time and tell me their problems. Sometimes they'd tell me that they were being picked on or bullied at school, and I'd always reply with the same advice. Tell a teacher and your mum and dad. Make sure you get help. Don't try and handle it on your own. I knew that was exactly what *I* should be doing, but I didn't.

For the first time I realised that things weren't always that easy. I didn't want to tell Mum for starters. It was so important to her that I fulfil my contract on *Hollywood High* which meant finishing my six weeks at Beaumont; she'd made that pretty clear the other day when she refused to take me home straightaway. Telling her how hard things were might get me home a bit faster, but it wouldn't make her happy. And I hadn't seen her really happy – at least not with me – since we'd arrived in Hollywood.

I just wanted her to see that I hadn't given up and that any decisions I made about my future were after I had tried my very best. And besides, it wasn't as if I would be going to Beaumont forever. I just had to keep holding on and I thought that I'd be strong enough to do that.

Then on the second Monday after the reviews came and Adrienne started hating me, something else happened. I was in English Class when Marianne Green opened the classroom door and exchanged a few words with Ms Martinez.

"Ruby?" Ms Martinez said, looking up at me. "Please can you go with Ms Green to the school office? You are excused from lessons until recess."

"Finally, they're deporting her," Adrienne said to a raft of giggles, all of which were quieted by a very stern stare from Ms Martinez. I got up, glancing at Tina as I left. I wondered what on earth warranted me being called to the office. My best guess was the shampoo all over my coursework. I'd copied it out again as best as I could, but it definitely wasn't as good as it had been the first time. Maybe they were worried I wasn't keeping up with my studies from home.

"So, Ruby," Ms Green asked me as I walked alongside her. "How are things going now for you? Are you still enjoying your stay with us?"

"Yes," I said, and I was only half lying. Maybe I did hate what the Adrienne brigade did to me every day, but I liked hanging out with Tina and Hunter, and I had even been to a couple of theatre-club meetings which gave me a chance to forget about everything else. I still loved acting, whether I was any good at it or not.

"I heard that some of the girls were giving you a tough time," Ms Green said, and then I thought that this must be what she wanted to see me about and I was relieved because it was less scary than falling behind on my homework.

"Oh, well, you know what us girls are like. We're always falling out. We'll be best friends again by this time next week." That was a full one hundred per cent lie.

"I think it's a bit more than girls falling out," Ms Green said, nodding at one of the blown-up pictures of me that had appeared since last recess. "Look, Ruby, you can talk to me without having to be afraid. Tell me who is leading this intimidation campaign against you and I'll deal with them, no matter how important they think they are. We do not tolerate that kind of behaviour from anyone in this school."

"I'm fine, honestly," I said as we stopped outside her office. "Can I go now?"

"Pardon?" Ms Green looked perplexed. "Oh no, sorry, Ruby, that wasn't why I called you out of class. Mr Blenheim and your mother are here for a meeting."

"Mr Blenheim?" I repeated. "A meeting about *Hollywood High*?"

"I think so," Ms Green said, dropping her gaze from mine as she showed me into her office where Mum and Mr Blenheim were waiting. I realised at once from the look on Mum's face when I went in what the meeting was really about.

It was sort of obvious really that they'd cut my part from the show. After all, their leading actress hated my guts, the critics loathed me and in the last few days, try as I might, I hadn't been able to concentrate properly on anything. So I shouldn't have been surprised, but I was.

"Look, Ruby," Mr Blenheim told me sadly, "this is as hard for me as it is for you. We took a gamble casting you and it's just not working out the way we hoped. So we're releasing you from the contract under the terms agreed with your agent. And you might as well know that the producers and I have decided to cut your role completely from season two. We're going to call a hiatus to retool the scripts and storyline and launch the season a little later than we planned."

I looked at Mum, but for once she didn't seem to know what to say. She reached over and put her hand on top of mine. "Can you just explain to us exactly why you're doing this?" she asked Mr Blenheim, while looking at me. "Is it because my daughter isn't good enough?"

He thought for a moment before answering.

"I run a business, Mrs Parker. And in business it's all about money. And the way things are now, Ruby doesn't add value to the show. If anything, she risks devaluing it. It's nothing personal and if it makes you feel any better Suzie is furious with me for caving in under the pressure of our financiers. For the record, my daughter thinks you are very talented, Ruby. But we have to think of the bigger picture. It's as simple as that."

There was a short but intense silence.

"It's OK," I said to Mum. "Actually it's good because now at least I can go home."

"We'll talk about that later, Ruby," Mum said.

"What's to talk about?" I asked her, surprised. "I don't have any reason to stay now, do I?"

My mum looked at me, a look which told me that when she said we'd talk about it later she meant it. I could tell that she was fuming inwardly and I didn't want that anger directed at me.

"I'll be contacting my lawyers, Mr Blenheim," she said. "To double-check that you can do this."

"I understand," Mr Blenheim said, "but I think you'll find there's nothing that you can do."

"Please can I come home with you now then?" I asked her, trying hard not to sound like I was pleading.

She shook her head. "No I'll pick you up after classes. You haven't been dropped from school, Ruby."

Mr Blenheim and my mum said stiff goodbyes to each other and then Mum took me to one side as I waited to go back to class. "You know that this isn't about you, don't you?" she said, and I could see she thought by saying that she was actually helping me. "It's all to do with politics and money and studio infighting, not about whether you can act."

"Yes," I replied uncertainly. "But... well, Mum, it is a little bit about me – it has to be. I mean, I *want* it to be about me now. I want to be able to go home, that's what *I* want. What's the point of staying at school here now?"

Mum gave me a quick hug. "We'll talk later," she told me.

I think I was in shock when I walked back into class. Perhaps Adrienne had something to do with it, but I don't think it would have taken very much more for the studio to make their mind up about me after those terrible reviews and the drop in box-office takings after the first weekend. I don't think I had ever felt so rejected in my whole life before.

Rejected by Danny, and even by my dad who I hadn't spoken to in weeks. And now rejected by Hollywood. I came here thinking of myself as a film star. I was leaving as a nobody. Not a normal person who still has all their hopes and dreams to follow, but as an actual, literal nobody who'd followed her dreams and had them crushed before her eyes. The thought of it made me feel lost and sad.

If I didn't have my dreams and hopes any more – then what did I have?

Chapter Eighteen

"I've been thinking," Mum said in the car when she picked me up after school. "About what's best for you and for your career. And I've decided we're not going home yet."

"But Mum," I protested in disbelief, "why wait around another two weeks – why?"

"Now, don't go crazy – but I'm thinking that we'll stay more like another couple of months. Don't you see, Ruby? You can't leave Hollywood in total disgrace, dropped by your TV show and with terrible reviews. If you leave like this you might never be able to come back."

"I don't want to come back!" I told her.

"You're saying that now because you're upset," Mum went on. "But it won't be like this every day. In a few weeks you'll be fine and will want another chance, I know you will. Besides, Ruby, I believe in you. I believe in your talent. I refuse to let your first trip to Hollywood end like this. I'm going to get back out there and line you up some auditions. It'll be hard, but we'll do it and I'm sure Jeremy can help."

"The last thing I want is to be offered parts because of who I know," I said. "That's what got me into this mess in the first place. Don't you get it, Mum? I'm not good enough."

"You're wrong." Mum shook her head.

We sat in silence as Mum pulled into the drive that led to Jeremy's house.

"Are you sure that's why you want me to stay?" I asked as she pulled up and turned off the engine. She looked at me, puzzled.

"What do you mean?"

"Do you want me to stay because you 'believe in me' or do you want me to stay because *you* want to stay? So you can live here with Jeremy in his nice house and drive his nice car and go shopping whenever you want and do stupid things to your hair and face. I don't think it's me you want, Mum. I think it's Hollywood."

"Ruby Parker, how dare you say that!" Mum roared.

I scrambled out of the car, slammed the door shut and headed for the front door where David raced out to greet me, yapping at my heels. Mum was right behind me.

"You know what? It *is* nice to be with Jeremy. I like living here with him. But I am a person too, Ruby, and I deserve a life of my own!" I tried to open the door with my key, but Mum stopped me. "But nothing is as important to me as you are. Everything I do is for you. And that's why we are staying. You'll be grateful in the long run."

She opened the door and I ran upstairs to my room and threw myself on the bed. I expected to be crying, but I wasn't. I was furious. I had never been so angry in all of my life.

And that's when I decided: I didn't care what Mum said. I was going home anyway.

Later that night, when Mum and Jeremy were downstairs, I crept out of my bedroom along the hall to Mum's room. It was hard to creep because David insisted on coming with me, taking one or two hesitant steps behind me as I tiptoed along the hall, looking up at me with quizzical eyes. I expected him to break my cover at any second, but he must have sensed the need to sit quiet because he didn't make a sound.

I knew exactly what I was looking for. I went over to the dressing table and opened and closed both the drawers, holding my breath as I searched. I was terrified that someone might hear or come in and discover me. I went over to the bedside table and carefully pulled it open. Inside was what I was looking for – my passport and our open return tickets. I picked up my ticket and looked at it for a moment. Was I really going to do this? Was I really going to do the most rebellious and stupid thing that I had ever done in my life?

I wavered and thought about putting the ticket back, about trying to talk to Mum again. But a swell of anger and hurt rose up in my chest and I thought, *What's the point of talking to Mum? She never listens to me any more. No one ever cares about what I think or what I need. I have to look after myself.*

So I took my passport and my ticket out of the drawer and covered Mum's up with some jewellery so that she wouldn't notice they were missing straightaway.

Next came the really nerve-wracking bit. I hid the ticket and passport in my room and, knowing I couldn't have David follow me this time, shut him in my bathroom.

"I'm sorry, boy," I told him. "It's only for a few minutes, OK?"

He started barking as soon as I closed the door, but David was always barking at something so I hoped nobody would notice and I crept downstairs. I could hear Mum and Jeremy talking.

"She's so young," Jeremy was saying. "A break wouldn't do her any harm. Child actors who rest and then come back to it later can do so well. Look at Drew Barrymore and Christian Bale."

"She's my daughter, Jeremy," Mum said crossly. "I know what I'm doing."

"I'm just saying that perhaps it wouldn't do any harm to take her home for a few weeks. Let everything calm down a bit."

I could see Mum's bag on the table by the door. To reach it I'd have to cut across behind where she and Jeremy were sitting. If either one of them happened to glance over their shoulders, they'd catch me in the act. I dropped to my knees and crawled along behind the sofa, hoping that Marie or Augusto wouldn't suddenly appear.

As I reached the table I felt along its surface until I got hold of Mum's bag, but I pulled the strap too hard so that it almost fell to the floor. I caught it just in time. Sitting on the floor and feeling sick with guilt I searched her bag. I slipped her wallet out and tucked it in my pocket. All I needed now was to get back upstairs unseen.

On the crawl back I noticed that Mum and Jeremy had stopped talking.

Back in my room, with a furious David released from his imprisonment, I opened Mum's purse and took out her credit cards.

Then I logged on to the airline website and checked their policy for minors travelling alone. It was fine, almost too easy. If you were over twelve and travelling alone, you didn't even need any special treatment, just for a parent to inform the airline.

I took a deep breath and called the reservation line.

"Hello," I said, lowering my voice. "My name is Janice Parker and I'd like to book the return part of a journey for my daughter, Ruby Parker. She is thirteen and will be travelling alone."

"And when would you like to book the ticket, madam?" the lady on the other end of the phone asked me.

"The first flight you have," I told her. "I don't mind which time."

Before I knew it I was booked on the 10.25 p.m. flight out of LAX the next evening. I put the phone down and waited for my heart to slow down, but it didn't.

Now, all I had to do was work out how to get to the airport without anybody noticing I had gone, at least, not until the flight was in the air. I looked in Mum's purse, my stomach churning. I'd need money for a cab and I didn't think I had enough of my own. So I took all the dollars I could out of her purse. I hid them and my ticket and passport in the lining of my pillow.

Tucking Mum's wallet back in my pocket I went downstairs and sneaked it back into her bag, relieved to see that she and Jeremy were no longer within earshot.

I went to bed after that, but I didn't sleep and not just because David kept on biting my toes.

"You know what, David," I said, picking him up and looking at him in his beady little eyes. "I'll actually quite miss you. Maybe you can get a pet passport and fly out for a visit some time? My cat would hate you and you would hate my cat, but I'd love to set you on Jade Caruso one day."

David growled at me uncertainly. Animals are supposed to have a sixth sense. They are supposed to know when something bad is going to happen, like an earthquake or a tidal wave. At that minute I was sure David knew that what I was planning was dangerous and foolhardy, which was why it was a good job he couldn't talk.

David might be worried about me, but I was terrified. I couldn't believe what I was doing. But I knew I had to do it. I had to get away from this place. I had to get home to a place where I could just be me again, and where being me would be enough.

What else could I do if my own mother wouldn't listen to me?

Dear Hunter and Tina,

I'm really sorry that you are going to get this note after I've gone and that I didn't get a proper chance to say goodbye to you.

Tina, you are a really cool girl and I would have liked to have had more time to get to know you properly. I'm really sorry for how I acted when I first came to Beaumont.

Hunter, you've been so kind to me, sticking by me and even asking me to the dance. I would have really liked to go to a Valentine's dance with you. But I can't stay any longer, I just can't.

Maybe I'll see you again sometime.

Love
Ruby x

Chapter Nineteen

It was raining in London when the plane landed. My mind was all muddled up and my stomach contracted as the plane taxied into the airport. I half expected to be arrested the minute the plane touched down, but then I thought it was too soon. Mum might have found the note by now that read, "Sorry, Mum, I had to go. Don't worry about me, I'll be fine. Love Ruby." But it would take her a while to find out any more than that.

And as for what would happen when she did realise what I'd done? Well, I hadn't thought that far ahead. All I thought about was getting a cab, finding my way through the huge and frightening airport when all I usually did was follow Mum around and do what she told me.

Once I was on the plane I felt like my life had been put into suspended animation for those long hours. I didn't worry, I didn't think, I didn't even care any more about how much trouble I would be in. I just ate snacks and watched films, wishing that I could go to sleep.

When I walked out of the airport and into the damp London evening I felt dazed and muddled by jet lag, and I was very tired because it felt like I hadn't slept for days. I asked someone what the time was and adjusted my watch. It was just after eight in the evening. I went over to the line of black cabs and the first one in the queue rolled his window down.

"Where to, love?"

I had to think for a moment, then I gave him my mum's address. After all, I had a key. I'd be fine on my own.

But when I got to our house I'd forgotten that I only had dollars and not enough of them to pay the cab driver even if he did accept foreign currency, which he told me quite crossly that he didn't.

I burst into tears because I was tired and scared and a nervous wreck. Luckily the sight of my tears made him kinder. "Anyone who can help you out?" he asked me.

"My dad?" I suggested reluctantly, and he drove me round there.

When I got out of the cab I was nervous. This wasn't exactly how I wanted to see my dad again for the first time in ages. Turning up on his doorstep a runaway and asking him for fifty pounds to pay a cab. But I didn't have any choice.

I pressed the bell and waited. Dad opened the door.

"Oh, Ruby!" he exclaimed, hugging me tightly. "Oh, thank God you are safe. Oh, thank God!"

And then my dad was crying which made me cry again. And it took both of us quite a while to sort ourselves out and pay the cabbie, by which time the fare had gone up another six pounds.

And the minute I saw Dad all my nerves went out of the window. I was just glad to be with him again.

"What on earth did you think you were doing?" Dad asked as he sat me down and handed me a cup of hot chocolate. I had heard him on the phone to Mum in the kitchen, telling her I was safe and with him. She must have wanted to talk to me, but Dad said, "I think it's best if you calm down, Janice. She's fine. That's the main thing. Talk to her when you get here."

"Your mum phoned me a couple of hours ago to tell me you had run away," Dad told me. "She was worried sick, Ruby. They had the police out looking for you. They've only just found that you booked a flight home and that you boarded it safely. It had landed before they could get anyone to the airport. I was waiting here *hoping* that this is where you would come. I don't understand, Ruby. This isn't like you at all."

"No one listened to me," I told him as I sipped my drink. "Mum didn't listen to me. I wanted to come home,

Dad. And for once in my life I thought I'd do what I wanted."

"I'm sure your mum was trying to do the best for you, Ruby," Dad chided me gently.

"But she wouldn't *listen* to me," I repeated wearily. "All I wanted to do was to come home. I didn't want Hollywood, or film stardom, or any of that. I don't want any of it any more, Dad. I've decided and I really mean it. I ran away because I was trying to get Mum, you and everybody else to take me seriously. I mean it – I'm through with acting."

"Well," Dad said, hugging me, "the main thing is that you're safe and now your mum knows you're safe. She was crying when I told her, Ruby. She's coming back on the first flight she can. She'll be here first thing in the morning. We will all talk then."

"I'm sorry I was rude to Denise, Dad," I told him, leaning my head on his shoulder and suddenly feeling exhausted.

"Were you?" Dad sounded puzzled. "Denise never mentioned anything. And anyway, I'm sorry that I haven't called you more. I got cross and confused, but I hope you know how much I love you, Rubes, even if I'm not the perfect dad."

"I loved that top you gave me for Christmas," I told

him sleepily. "I'm wearing it – look."

"It suits you, love," Dad said. "Now try to get some sleep and we'll sort everything out tomorrow when your mum gets here."

"And you promise you'll listen to me?" I mumbled almost asleep.

"I promise," Dad said.

Chapter Twenty

"But you have to come," Nydia said firmly, trying to pull me up off my bed.

"No, I don't," I replied, yanking my arm from hers. "I can't think of one good reason why I should go to the Academy's Valentine disco to be a gooseberry. Anne-Marie will have Sean, you'll have Greg, and Danny will have 'Me-lo-dy'."

I said Danny's new girlfriend's name in the same high-pitched squeaky voice that me and Anne-Marie always did. Nydia, while not actually befriending her, wouldn't be openly mean about her, so she didn't join in.

"Plus, I've had the worst reviews ever written about anybody *and* I got dropped from *Hollywood High*. Why would I want to face Jade and Menakshi now when half-term's coming up? I'm grateful I've been allowed time off as it is. The longer it is until I have to see those two and their cronies, the better. In fact, if I never have to see them again, that would be fine…" I trailed off.

There was something I had to tell Anne-Marie and Nydia that I hadn't yet, something that I couldn't quite bring myself to say.

"But you have to come!" Nydia said urgently.

"Look, you can wear this." Annie Marie threw a red dress on the bed. It was one that Mum had brought back from Hollywood along with all of the stuff I'd left behind.

When Mum had arrived at Dad's flat the day after I ran away, it had been strange to see her again because the Mum that turned up that day wasn't the Mum that I ran away from. She looked like herself again, as if she'd left the Hollywood version of herself checked in at the airport.

"Oh, Ruby!" she said crossly, before crying and hugging me. "You stupid, stupid girl! I'm so sorry!"

We talked for a long time in Dad's living room, the three of us. When I saw how worried and upset I'd made Mum, I realised for the first time how terribly dangerous what I had done was and how easy it would have been for something really bad to happen to me. And then I sort of got scared, even though there wasn't anything to be scared of any more, and I cried. I cried and cried and cried. It wasn't just because I'd frightened myself, but also because with my mum and dad's arms around me at last, I *could* cry properly about everything that had happened to me. And a lot had happened.

I felt as if I'd been trodden on a million times by a million people wearing two million stomping boots. When you're thirteen it's easy to feel bad about yourself. If your skin's broken out or your hair's all wrong or if you haven't got the right outfit or friends, it can feel as if the world is ending. But nothing could compare to the total and utter humiliation I faced in Hollywood. If ever I'm feeling a bit fat or frumpy or bored or grumpy again, I'm just going to remind myself about that time. The time when I got completely squished and it felt as if the whole world was watching. Because everything that happened to me out there has changed me. It's changed me for good.

And now that I am changed, I have decided what to do. After Mum and Dad and I talked they agreed to back my decision, even though they didn't like it or agree with it, because they'd both promised to listen to me and what I wanted, and I would not change my mind.

Mum said she was moving back into our house with me and Everest and that was where she was planning to stay from now on, with Jeremy visiting when he can. Dad told me he was decorating his flat next weekend along with his so-called... with Denise and asked me if I'd like to help them pick colours.

Dad wasn't even that cross with me any more. He said that probably if he'd been a better dad, he would have called me when I was in Hollywood instead of sulking. He said now I was growing up I had to realise that we are all only human – adults too. And he asked me if I'd forgive him.

I pretended to think about it for a second just to make him laugh and then I hugged him tight.

It was a funny and a hard thing to realise: that Mum and Dad sometimes got things wrong. That all three of us had got things wrong recently, but that it didn't mean we didn't love or need each other just as much as always.

"No matter what," Mum had said to us on the day she came back, "you and me and Dad, we're still a family. That will never change. And if you ever think that either of us are forgetting that, then you have to tell us, OK?"

"OK," I said. And that's when I told them my decision.

"I'm not wearing that," I said, looking at the red dress. It was one I got free after I appeared on *The Carl Vine Show* and it reminded me too much of everything that had happened.

"Oh, so you *are* coming then, if we can find something you like?" Nydia asked me. I was puzzled.

"Look, Nydia, you are a really good, kind and sweet friend to try and make me come to the dance," I told her, "but I know you'd rather be alone with Greg – and that's fine. I'll be OK here. I have chocolates and a DVD."

"Right, how about this then?" Anne-Marie said, throwing a pale-blue dress with diamante around the neckline on the bed. "This one would be *perfect*."

"Perfect for what?" I exclaimed. "Perfect for standing about on my own watching my ex dance to his own single with Me-lod-y?"

"Listen to me," Anne-Marie said, sitting on my bed and putting her face close to mine. "There comes a time in every girl's life when she has to make a stand. When she has to show Jade and Menakshi, Danny and Me-lod-y and the rest, that she's still standing tall. That Hollywood chucked all it could at her and that, even though her boyfriend chucked her for some drippy chick too, she isn't beaten because she is still tough and cool and ready to party! You *have* to go to the dance, Ruby. You *have* to show them that you're still alive!"

Nydia applauded and I thought about what I had to tell them and hadn't quite been able to yet. Anne-Marie's speech might have only been a ploy to get me to go with them, but she did have a point. I didn't want anyone to think that what I planned to do was cowardly. I wanted them all to see I was doing it for me, because it was the right thing to do. Not because I was scared.

"OK then, I'll go," I said, feeling the knots in my tummy tighten.

"Oh what a relief," Nydia said, hugging me. "This is going to be so cool!"

"Nydia, chill," Anne-Marie told her firmly. "It's a school dance, not the Oscars. She looked me up and down. "Right then, let's get you ready."

The Valentine's dance was being held in the main hall of the Academy. Unlike the one that was planned for Beaumont which had had a decorations committee and live music planned, the hall was decorated with some disco lights and a few balloons that were being kicked around the floor by some boys. It was already full of people when we arrived and I found myself stuck in the doorway, not quite able to make myself walk into the hall full of students who I knew would all be thinking the same thing about me: *loser*.

"Go on, Rubes," Nydia said encouragingly, holding my hand. "You look great!"

But it was Anne-Marie's firm shove in the small of my back that finally got me to move through the door.

I could feel everybody's eyes as I walked into the room and I wasn't sure if Anne-Marie's arm, now firmly linked through mine, was for support or to stop me bolting.

"Be strong," she said in my ear. "Nobody will say anything to your face because if they do, I'll deck 'em."

"That's a comfort," I said to my friend, who looked like an angel, but had the venom of a vengeful cobra when provoked. "But it's more what they are saying behind my back I'm worried about." I thought about Tina. "It's horrible to know that people are talking about you, even if you can't hear what they are saying."

"Just block it out," Anne-Marie instructed me as she spotted Sean over the other side of the room and treated him to a dazzling smile. "Focus on being fabulous. So what if you are washed out in Hollywood – you still look great in that dress."

"Ladies," Sean said, greeting us as we approached. Nydia's boyfriend Greg, who I hadn't met but who I had heard A LOT about, was with him. His face lit up when he saw Nydia.

It was then that I realised what good friends I had. How many other girls would have forsaken being picked up for the Valentine's dance by boyfriends bearing flowers just so that they could drag their sad and broken, rubbish friend along with them in a futile bid to cheer her up?

Suddenly I felt a bit of a wobble about my so far still secret plans. I wondered if I was doing the right thing after all? Maybe there was something to be said for just staying the same. Except that after what happened to me in Hollywood I wasn't the same any more, and if I wasn't the same, then how could anything else be?

Besides, good friends are friends whatever happens. And nothing could change that for me, Nydia and Anne-Marie, no matter where we were in the world. I was sure of that.

We stood around sipping fruit-juice cocktails for a while, Nydia deliberately not holding hands with Greg, and Anne-Marie shooting evil stares at anyone who dared even glance in our direction. I was starting to relax and even to enjoy myself. Greg was pretty funny and Sean was always entertaining, especially with Anne-Marie as his perfect foil.

I was on the point of agreeing to dance with the girls when Danny walked in, with Melody on his arm. My heart sank like a brick. It was the first time I had laid eyes on him since I had got his letter and I was disappointed to see that he was still the Danny I missed. He hadn't been avoiding me. If anything, it was the other way around because he had called me a few times on my mobile. But each time I rejected the call because I decided I was depressed enough without having to listen to him saying things like, "We can still be friends" and "It's me, not you". And besides, I'm only thirteen. I don't have to be mature about relationship break-ups until I'm at least seventeen. So I ignored him.

But he was a lot easier to ignore when I couldn't see him or Melody. Or him with Melody. And now here they both were, looking like the perfect Valentine's couple, Danny in a black suit, black shirt and tie, and Melody in a red dress with black polka dots and glossy golden hair. Cow.

"I think I might go," I said, dropping my gaze as Danny spotted me looking at him. But both Anne-Marie and Nydia clutched my arms and held me still.

"You can't go," Nydia said.

"Look, I've arrived and people have seen me and they know I'm not dead of shame so..." I tried to move but Nydia actually stood in front of me, barring my way.

"You are not going," she said, biting her lip because she was not the most confident bossy person in the world. "Please, Rubes. Just wait ten more minutes and if you still want to go then, that's fine."

"What difference does ten more minutes make?" I asked.

"Listen," Anne-Marie said, mingling a smile and a mildly threatening tone perfectly. "You're staying till I say you can go – got it?"

"But *why*?" I asked. No one answered.

It was just as Danny, with his relentless determination to be good friends with me, was bringing Melody over in our direction that the lights dimmed and the DJ put the first soppy song of the night on. My eyes met Danny's and for a split second we looked at each other before his eyes turned to Melody. As they began to sway, other couples paired off, even ones who weren't going out with each other, and I felt like I was the only girl in the whole world who had no one to dance with on Valentine's day.

"You can dance with Sean if you like," Anne-Marie offered as Sean swept her by.

"No," I shook my head. "I'm fine. You two dance. I'm waiting for my ten minutes to be up."

As they slowly turned around, I caught Nydia smiling at Anne-Marie and I couldn't think what they found so funny about their best friend standing about, chucked and alone on Valentine's night.

That was when I felt the tap on my shoulder.

I turned round.

My jaw dropped and if I hadn't been rigid with shock I would have fainted.

Hunter was standing before me in a tuxedo and bow tie holding a red rose in his hand.

"Ruby, may I have this dance?" he asked me, offering me the rose.

"May you... I mean... is it...? Are you... Hunter?" I struggled to speak because he was the very last person in the whole world that I expected to see here at this precise moment and for a second I feared that I had gone barking mad.

"You're *here*," I said in disbelief.

"Yes, I'm here," Hunter told me with a slow smile. "Because when I say I'm taking a girl to a Valentine's dance, I mean it, even if I have to cross the Atlantic to do it." He grinned at me. "And because it just so happened that the studio is bringing some of the cast over to promote the show here. When I found out, I asked my mom if we could come a few days early and luckily for me she was happy to spend an extra weekend shopping in London."

"I can't believe it!" I said, starting to laugh. I took the rose from Hunter's hand. "But I'm glad you're here, Hunter. I'm really, really pleased to see you."

"Does that mean you'll dance with me?" Hunter asked again. "Or should we stand here all night so that all your schoolfriends can stare at us?"

"Let's dance," I said happily.

Hunter was right; everyone was watching us, but this time I didn't care. This time I wanted them to watch me because I was the only girl who was dancing with a mysterious, handsome stranger. It was like a dream. No, better than that, it was like the end of a film and I was the heroine.

Then I saw Nydia and Anne-Marie's faces and I knew that was why they had been so keen to get me to come to the dance. They had known about Hunter's arrival all along.

I swirled around with Hunter to the slow dances and was twirled around by him to the quick ones until I was giddy. Jade and Menakshi looked completely disgusted, which was good enough, but even better, nobody in the UK knew who Hunter was yet. So right now we could stop being Ruby Parker Failed Actress and Hunter Blake Rising Superstar and just be Ruby and Hunter, two kids at the school disco.

Hunter had gone to get me some juice when Anne-Marie dug me in the ribs and whispered in my ear, "Look at Danny."

I glanced over and found that Danny was watching me, his face covered in stormy clouds. Although what he had to be cross about I couldn't imagine. He had dumped me, after all.

"Typical," Anne-Marie said, rolling her eyes. "It's fine for him to swan off with Me-lod-y, but when you turn up with a handsome hunk of a boy he's all moody and jealous on you."

I looked at Danny for a moment longer and then, shrugging my shoulders, turned my back on him. What was the point in worrying about him now?

"You two were in on it, weren't you?" I asked Anne-Marie and Nydia who had come over to join us. "You knew all the time that Hunter was planning to come to the school dance – but how? How did he even know about it?"

"We thought you needed something *big* to cheer you up, so that you'd feel OK about coming back to school," Anne Marie said. "When you got back and told us about everything that happened over there, *including* Hunter asking you out, it got us thinking – what could we do?"

"And then," Nydia joined in, "I saw in *Teen Girl!* that the cast of *Hollywood High* were coming over at the end of February to do promos with T4, including Hunter."

"We remembered that you'd e-mailed us from school and that you had a Beaumont e-mail address, so we tried working out Hunter's e-mail address from that, but it was harder than it seemed. It took four goes," Anne-Marie said. "Well, four goes until the e-mail didn't bounce back to us as unknown. We still didn't know if we had the right address or, if we did, if he'd even reply to us."

"But we called the e-mail 'Want to Take Ruby Parker to the Dance?' and funnily that made Hunter read it!"

Nydia giggled and I blushed of course. "We told Hunter about the disco and how we thought it would really cheer you up, and once we managed to persuade him that you actually would be happy to see him, he organised the rest."

Anne-Marie put an arm around me and kissed me on the cheek. "So now you don't have to worry about all the stuff that happened over there any more because you're the girl with the secret hot boyfriend!"

"You can thank us now if you like," Nydia said happily.

"Thank you," I said, feeling suddenly nervous and sad about what I had to tell them. "You two are the best friends in the world! I really mean that!"

The three of us hugged and I realised that this was the moment. I had to tell them now.

"It really would have been the coolest way to make a comeback here," I said.

"I know," Nydia said. "Now after half term it will be all 'Oooh, Ruby, who *was* that mysterious boy you were kissing...?'"

"I haven't kissed him!" I exclaimed, glancing over at Hunter as he joked around with Sean and Greg.

"Yet," Anne-Marie said, rolling her eyes. "And then *Hollywood High* will be on TV over here and he'll be famous and everybody will be talking about you for the right reasons again."

"They won't," I said steadily.

"Yes, they will. They will die of jealousy because—"

"They won't," I said, a little more firmly so that my friends stopped talking and started listening. "Look, I have to tell you something."

"What?" Nydia asked me cautiously.

"I'm not coming back to the Academy after half term," I told them. "I'm starting at the comprehensive instead."

"You..."

"*What?*" Nydia exclaimed. "But, Ruby, why?"

"Is it your parents?" Anne-Marie asked me intently. "Are they forcing you?"

"No!" I exclaimed. "No. Look, something dawned on

me while all the horrible stuff was going on. I like acting, I love acting and I've been lucky. So lucky that I started to believe I was good enough at it to be a real star – like Imogene or Jeremy. But I'm not. I'm just a girl who likes to play-act. The last few weeks have proved that. I'm not good enough to be at the Academy, I don't deserve my place. So I'm leaving. I'm starting at Highgate Comp."

Nydia and Anne-Marie stared at me open mouthed.

"But you can't…" Nydia said.

"It won't make any difference to us," I went on, determined not to waver. "I'll see you all the time after school and at weekends, just not here." I stopped and looked around the school hall where I had had so many great, boring, important and fun times.

My friends were both silent.

"Look," I went on smiling at them so they would know I was happy, "remember that speech that Ms Lighthouse gives us at the beginning of every term? The one when she says that to be an actor you need grit and determination and the will to never give up, unless you know that you must give up because you aren't good enough?"

They both nodded, glancing at each other.

"Well I know that now," I said. "I'm not good enough

to act professionally. I want to be like Sean. If I do any acting again, I want it to be for fun without any of the pressure or the worry. And seriously, if Mum and Dad and Sylvia Lighthouse herself can't talk me out of it, then neither can you."

"But you are good enough to be a star. You're brilliant," Nydia said. "The best out of all of us."

I shook my head. "But don't you see, Nydia, even if I am, I don't want it any more. They have a good drama club at Highgate. Who knows, I might even get the lead in the school play for once and you can all come and see me!"

There was silence as my friends tried to take in what I had said.

"Look," I said, hugging them both as Hunter returned and handed me a drink, "let's not be sad. We're at a party and this is a new beginning! It's going to be fantastic!"

"If it's really what you want..." Nydia said sadly.

"Then we'll have to put up with it," Anne-Marie added. "Even if we think you are wrong."

"Friends forever?" I asked them. The three of us hugged tightly.

"Friends forever," we chorused.

Then the music slowed down again and couples began to pair off around us.

Just as Hunter picked up my hand to lead me to the dance floor, Danny suddenly appeared. "Ruby," he said, "I've been meaning to talk to you."

"Have you?" I said stiffly. "Well, why don't you write me a letter? You're good at those."

"I'm sorry," Danny persisted, "about how everything happened. I—"

"Danny," I said making myself sound much harder and cooler than I felt, "do you mind? I'm dancing with my boyfriend."

I led Hunter on to the dance floor and made myself not look at where I could still feel Danny was standing.

"Sorry I said you were my boyfriend," I told Hunter when we were out of earshot.

"Don't apologise," Hunter said, with half a smile. "Do you think that I came all this way to dance with just any old girl? I was kind of hoping you would be my girlfriend before I left."

I stopped dancing and looked up at Hunter. "I can't," I said.

"What?" he looked surprised. "But why?"

"Because you're here for one weekend, and because you're a megastar and I'm not even an actor any more. I'm leaving this school and going to a normal one. No more trips to Hollywood, no more auditions or scripts to learn ever again. And you can't go out with some nobody from nowhere. Your publicist would die."

"I could actually," Hunter said. "But I wouldn't have to because you aren't a nobody, you're you. And it's you I like, Ruby."

I smiled at him and for a second I let myself imagine that everything could be different, I could date Hunter and go back to the Academy and have my old life back. But I knew it wasn't possible because I had changed too much. Hollywood had changed me.

"Hunter, you are so lovely and having you here tonight is wonderful. But trust me, our lives are not only going to be continents apart, they are going to be worlds apart."

Hunter watched me for a long moment. "OK, Ruby," he said a little sadly. "I can't make you be my girl. So I have just one last question to ask you."

"What's that?"

"How do you feel about kissing a guy who's not your boyfriend?"

"I think that would be fine," I said in a small, squeaky voice. I caught my breath and felt my cheeks glow.

And Hunter kissed me there under the twinkling disco lights with everybody watching us, and for a few seconds I thought that my toes were floating just above the ground. Anne-Marie and Nydia were right. What better way could there be to leave Sylvia Lighthouse's Academy for the Performing Arts?

This was my curtain call.

Chapter

Twenty-one

I looked at myself in the mirror. I was wearing my new school uniform. It wasn't any more flattering than the one I used to wear at the Academy, but I liked it more because it meant a new day and a new start. A clean page.

Downstairs, Mum was waiting for me with toast and tea. "Nervous?" she asked as I sat down and Everest positioned himself on the table, hopeful that he'd be able to swipe himself some toast.

I thought for a moment. "I'm not actually," I told her. "I probably should be. I mean, it's a massive school full of kids and I don't know any of them. But, well, starting a new school is what loads of girls my age do all the time. It's a scary thing to do, but at least it's normal. And I think I'm really going to like just being a normal nearly fourteen-year-old girl thinking about maths and history and home time."

"Some of the other children might tease you a bit because they'll know who you are," Mum warned me.

"I know," I said. "But once you've stood up to Adrienne Charles, you can stand up to anyone, so I'm not worried about that. I'll make friends."

"Of course you will," Mum said, sitting down and patting me on the back of the hand. "Ruby, I wanted to say that I'm sorry. I'm sorry if I let you down while we were away. If I got carried away and confused and forgot what my priorities are. I hope you know that all I want is for you to be happy."

"I do know that," I said. "And, well, um – I don't know what's going to happen next, I don't know what Highgate Comp will be like, the kind of people I'll meet there or anything like that. But I've got this funny feeling in my tummy, a feeling I've never had before, and it's telling me that whatever happens to me next, it's going to be pretty exciting. It's telling me that my hopes and dreams aren't over. They're only just beginning to come true."

I stood in the middle of the stage and looked out across the empty theatre, gold and ornate, beautiful and frightening all at the same time. But it didn't feel empty. It was as if all the plays and musicals had left something behind, like energy that vibrated in the air. It felt as if I was plugged into it and it was filling me with electricity.

Someone switched on a spotlight. It dazzled me for a minute and I had to shield my eyes for a second. Then I dropped my hand and tipped my face to the beam, feeling its warmth on my cheeks.

I've given up, I reminded myself sternly. I'm only here because I have to be, not because I'm good enough.

But there was something else that made me feel I might, just might, truly belong on that stage…

Coming soon

Ruby Parker

Stage Star

ROWAN COLEMAN

Catch up with all of Ruby's
celebrity adventures!

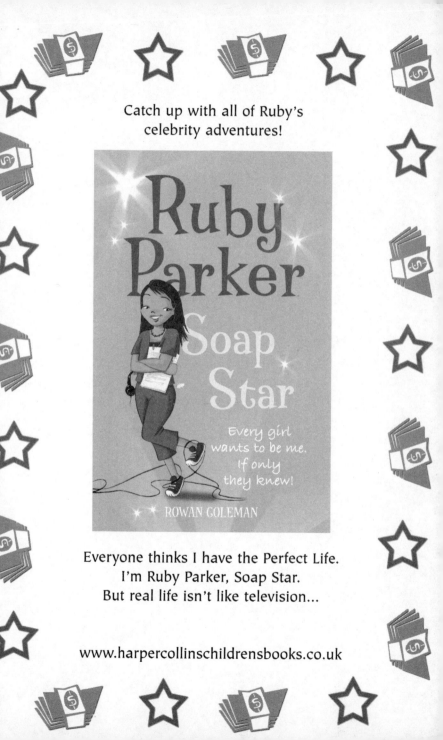

Everyone thinks I have the Perfect Life.
I'm Ruby Parker, Soap Star.
But real life isn't like television...

www.harpercollinschildrensbooks.co.uk

Catch up with all of Ruby's
celebrity adventures!

Ruby Parker Film Star

Wish me luck for my first audition!
★ ★ ROWAN COLEMAN

I used to be Ruby Parker, Soap Star.
Now I'm trying to be Ruby Parker, Movie Star.
But what if I turn out to be Ruby Parker,
No Use At All?

www.harpercollinschildrensbooks.co.uk